IN LOVE WITH AN EAST COAST MANIAC 3: GRIZZ AND SUNDAE

JAHQUEL J.

D1713437

—

**TEXT UCP TO 22828 TO SUBSCRIBE TO OUR
MAILING LIST**
**If you would like to join our team, submit the first 3‑4
chapters of your completed manuscript to**
Submissions@UrbanChaptersPublications.com

To all the mothers who have carried, but never carried your child home, my heart is with you. To my little one, I love you.

It's no coincidence that Pregnancy and Infant Loss Remembrance Day is October 15th, my birthday is October 15th and this book is releasing on October 15th.

A NOTE FROM THE AUTHOR:

This book put me through it. I worked so hard on this book, and I'm proud of the outcome of everybody. Some you may not understand, and some you'll love. In the end, everyone got their happy ending. I wrapped this book up, and there will not be a part four, five, or six. The next book that will come will be Paris McKnight's book. However, it will solely be about her and her problems. Her family will pop in from time to time, but this book will be about her ONLY.

I'm so excited about my next project, and it will be a stand-alone. I pray you guys love it because it will be different than my other reads! As always, I appreciate you all.

Make sure to join and follow me on all my social media to stay in loop of all things me!
Make sure you answer the questions asked!

A NOTE FROM THE AUTHOR:

www.facebook.com/JahquelJ
http://www.instagram.com/_Jahquel
http://www.twitter.com/Author_Jahquel
Be sure to join my reader's group on Facebook
www.facebook.com/ Jahquel's we reading or nah?

Make sure you join my newest group –
www.facebook.com/Babeswithbooks

UZI

Tweeti stood holding Taz's hand with black shades covering her puffy eyes. She sniffled and squeezed her son's hand gently as she stared at the gold casket that contained her husband's body. Tweeti didn't cry, speak, or look at anyone during the entire funeral. She requested that the burial only be attended by close family and friends. She stood there with her son and looked at the casket and turned her head to the side. I reached down and picked up Taz, and she stepped forward and touched the coffin. Everyone watched as the grieving widow went to say her last goodbyes before the coffin was lowered into the ground. Remi sniffled beside me and reached up to kiss Taz on the cheek.

"Bring him to say goodbye to his father, honey," she told me, and I stepped forward. Taz touched the coffin and then looked back at me. He leaned his head down on my shoulder, and I stepped back and allowed Tweeti her time with her husband.

My baby brother. The one who was supposed to outlive me was being buried in a box today.

"Baby, someone is knocking on the door like they lost their mind." Remi shook me out of my sleep. The dream I was having had my chest tight with fear. It wasn't the first time I dreamed about one of my siblings dying. It was something that I could never get used to. I wiped the sleep out my eyes, checked the clock on the night table, and stood up.

"Who the fuck stupid enough to knock on my shit at three in the morning," I grumbled as I grabbed my gun off the night table and headed downstairs. When I opened the bedroom door, Paris was standing there, confused. "Go back to bed," I told her.

"Um, Dad, I'm not going to sleep until I know you're back up these stairs safe," she protested like I knew she would. Where did the quiet and soft-spoken little girl go?

"Baby, she's right. We're coming behind you just in case," Remi co-signed.

"What the fuck the both of you going to do? Y'all acting like I never handled myself."

BOOM! BOOM!

"Oh hell nah. Who the hell banging on the door like that?" Remi bypassed me and headed down the stairs. I shoved her to the side and swung the door opened first and aimed my gun second. My gun was sitting on Peblo's lip when I finally looked from around the door.

"Peblo, what the fuck you doing knocking on my door at this time? I know you not coming around here for a fix, because I'll kill you on these steps," I threatened and put my gun away.

Peblo was that crackhead that everyone knew. It didn't matter where you were from, you knew who Peblo was. The little niggas around the way had made him an Instagram account, and he was insta-famous. Nigga was sponsoring Fashion Nova men and all that kind of shit. They broke bread with him, and he was one of the few crackheads that could say he got his money for his fix with honest money. He stood there with a linty black button up shirt, jean shorts, and sneakers that looked like he ran from hell and back in them.

On the plus side, he had a fresh haircut, and his lips didn't look like he been sucking dick and got nut busted on them, so that was a plus. Peblo used to work for the fire station. When 9/11 hit, he ended up going to help save people and got injured. As much as people wanted to sit and mourn about the people whose lives were taken, they forgot about the people who risked their lives to help those that were still living. Peblo was one of those people who used to be someone. Now all everyone saw him as was a crackhead who always looked like he had sucked some dick. Me and Jah appreciated the man he used to be and would always have respect for him. If I had ten minutes to sit and chat with him, I gave him that. Even in his current condition, he was wise.

"Nah, nah, nah... son, would never disrespect you like that. Your brother!" he hollered. "He was shot in his car by some man." He finally got the words out.

My entire body grew tense as I watched this man look as if he wanted to fall apart in front of me. "Some man shot him in his car. I called the cops, and he wasn't breathing when the ambulance whisked him away. It took me a while before I could remember where your house was. I was walking around for hours."

"Peblo, come in." I held the door opened, and he walked inside. He looked around, and his eyes widened. "I'm not gonna have shit missing, am I?"

"Not from me," he quickly assured me.

"What hospital did they take him to?" I went into the hall closet and pulled on a hoodie and pants. When you lived in the streets, you had to be prepared to go. I had clothes stashed all over this crib. You never knew when you had to dip out without a second thought. I kept telling Remi's ass this, and she insisted on leaving luggage around the crib. It wasn't the point I was trying to make, so I left the subject alone when it came to her.

"Mount Sinai Hospital," he replied in-between smacking. Remi had fixed him some leftovers, and he was smashing that shit down.

"Bet. Baby, I'll call you when I get there." When I turned around, I saw tears and worry in Remi's eyes. She was shaking as she held onto the side of the counter. Paris was rubbing her shoulders, and I walked over to her and kissed her on the forehead. "He's gonna be good."

"I don't think so. He got popped right in the head and in his legs. He didn't look good when they put him on that stretcher." Peblo's loud-mouthed ass smacked as reencountered what happened.

"I have to call Tweeti. I know they're going through it right now, but she needs to know." She put her hand over her mouth and shook in fear. "What if he's gone, babe?"

It was something I had been trying to talk myself out of thinking since Peblo arrived at my front door. Dead? Nah, my brother couldn't be dead. He had so much to live for, and God wasn't done with him yet.

"Nah, Jah got too much shit to talk. Let me find out what's going on, and I'll call you. Yo, Peblo, let's roll," I told him, and he grabbed the plate and followed behind me.

My Rolls Royce was parked outside, so we jumped inside. "This right here a fine automobile." Peblo admired the car as I sped out of my parking spot.

"Who shot him?" I needed to know everything because soon as I found out that my brother was good, I was painting this city fucking red until I had the nigga responsible for this shit.

"I didn't get to see, boss. He had on a hoodie... but I know he called me a crackhead."

"He saw you there?"

"Yes. He chuckled and said, 'who's going to believe a

crackhead'." He acted hurt like his ass wasn't in fact a crackhead.

"You can't think of anything that stood out about him?"

"Other than him calling me a crackhead?"

"Peblo!"

"No, boss. I can't think of anything." He sounded disappointed that he couldn't remember anything from the person that shot Jah.

"It's all good, Peblo," I assured him and continued to the hospital. My hands were shaking, and my heart was beating so hard that I was sure Peblo had heard it. I tried to remain that strong man that everyone relied on, but knowing that my baby brother could be taken from me had me scared as fuck. This was the second time he had been shot and we thought we were going to lose him. I couldn't lose my brother, best friend, and ace. He meant the world to me, and my life wouldn't be the same if he wasn't there with me.

Then, it wasn't even about me anymore. He had a son and wife that he needed to be here for too. Tweeti wouldn't be able to go on knowing that her husband was killed in cold blood in his car. How the fuck could sis move on knowing shit like that? Then, my nephew would have to grow up without his father. The shit hurt like hell when I thought about losing someone who meant the world to me. The shit felt like I was about to lose a parent or a child. My pops wasn't around much when we were growing up, so it was up to me to take control and teach Jah things. Sometimes I blamed myself for putting him onto the streets. He should have gone to college and did something other than trap. I had bigger plans for both him and Wynner. They were supposed to be better than me. I wanted Wynner to go to college, graduate, and start a business or have a career. Instead, my sister is the wife of an ex- drug dealer and a mother of two children.

She reminded me so much of my mother, and it wasn't a compliment.

We arrived at the hospital, and I parked in a handicap spot. If my shit was towed, I'd pay to get it out. Right now, my mind was on seeing if my brother was fine. Me and Peblo breezed through the front and went straight to the front desk.

"Yeah, a man just came in and he's bad... Girl, he might be dead the way he looked," one of the nurses was saying to the other.

"Ma'am!" I hollered. She had to be talking about Jah.

"Sir, you don't have to holler. I'm right here." She laughed and took a seat in her chair. "What's so urgent?" She batted her eyelashes and stared at me. I could tell she was flirting with me from the way her voice changed and got all soft.

"The man you were just speaking on?"

"Oh, he came in with GSW to the head and legs and chest," she informed me. "You know him or something?"

"He might be my brother."

She started pecking away at the computer and looked up at me. "What's his name? He'll be in the system because he had an ID on him."

"Jahquel McKnight."

"That name is so pr—"

"You think I give a fuck about what's pretty or not? I need to know if that's my fucking brother, and if you can't tell me, then I'll come back there and find out my damn self."

"I'm just saying," she replied. "Yes, it was him that was brought here. He's currently in surgery, but I'll let the doctor know that he has family waiting on him."

"How long has he been in surgery?"

"An hour. The doctor will be out to talk to you when he's out of surgery. Go to the third floor and turn left and there's a waiting area for the family," she told me and handed both me and Peblo a visitor's pass.

This shit had my chest hurting, and I felt like I was going to pass out. I was a strong nigga and took a lot of shit on the chin and moved on, but not my brother. It couldn't be my brother that was shot that many times and left in his car alone. Who the fuck was that bold to touch my brother? Niggas dreamed about knocking either one of us off, but none of them were brave enough to do that shit. Who the fuck was walking around my city and thought that they could touch me?

"Calm down." I felt a soft pair of hands reach up and touch my ears. When I turned around, it was Remi and Paris. "I know you, and I know that you're so strong for everyone else, and you need someone to be strong for you. I'm here." She hugged me.

"And I'm here too, Daddy," Paris joined the hug.

This is why I was going to marry this woman. She knew me like the back of her hand. How did she know I needed her the most right now? I was the rock for everyone, and every once in a while, I needed someone to lean on. I never complained or asked for someone to be there for me; however, Remi knew. I didn't need a woman with a fat ass, fly fashion, and fire head. I needed a woman that knew when to step in when I felt I was about to lose my shit. Remi had all those other things, but none of those things were important when you needed someone to be there emotionally.

"Ma'am, where should we wait?" Remi asked. The nurse now had an attitude and rambled off the instructions she had told me before. The same instructions that I had forgot because I was too far in my head.

"Boss, let me know how he turns out. I'm going to keep my ear to the streets," Peblo promised and headed toward the door.

I didn't expect for him to stick around, but I wasn't about to leave him in my crib with my fiancée and daughter, so telling him to come with me was the best thing I could think of in the moment. We made it to the third floor and took a seat in the waiting room. Remi held my hand and kissed it while staring at me.

"What are they saying?"

"The nurse told me he was shot in the head, leg, and chest," I replied, still not wanting to believe that it was my brother she was talking about.

"Oh my God. Not Uncle Jah." Paris gasped. I hated she had to witness all of this, but she had to know. I wasn't a fool and put my daughter onto game way before any other nigga could. She knew what her father did and what our family had our hands in.

"Baby girl, he's going to be fine," Remi assured her.

"Stop telling her that, babe. We don't know that." I stopped her. She was giving her false hope, and that doctor could come out and tell us that Jah was dead on that operation table.

"I believe in the man upstairs, and I know He wouldn't do this to Jah. You can believe what you want, but I'm going to pray to the same man that brought you into my life and helped me to live when I was shot. He hasn't failed me yet, and I know He won't when it comes to Jahquel," she told me and got up. "I'm going to grab something to drink. You want anything?"

"Nah." I sighed.

"Who is going to call Tweeti?" Paris brought up something I hadn't thought about since I walked into this hospital.

Remi stared at me. "Call her, babe. She needs to hear it from you," she told me and left out of the waiting room. I played with my phone in my hand and went over to the window to make a call that I knew wouldn't be easy.

✸ 2 ✸

TWEETI

The house phone never rang, so when I reached across and answered the phone, I was annoyed. Everyone knew that I turned my phone on silent when I went to bed. Taz loved to use any and every sound as an excuse to get up and use that as playtime.

With him beside me, I put the phone to my ear and whispered, "Hello?"

"Tweet, I need you to listen to me now. I'm sending the driver to come scoop you up and bring you to me."

"What the hell for? You know how long it took me to ge—"

"Jah has been shot, and he's in surgery," Uzi blurted out, and I sat all the way up in the bed. My heart started beating super-fast, and my breathing became shallow. "You there?"

"H... how did this happen? He called me not too long ago and said he'll be home soon," I whispered while holding the phone with a death grip.

"I'm trying to find all of that out now. What I need you to do is to get here quick," he told me, and I ripped the covers off of me.

"I'm coming." I sniffled and ran down to the guestroom where my mother was sleeping.

When I opened her door, she was watching some late-night show. Usually, she stayed up with Taz when he wouldn't go to sleep. Evelyn suffered from insomnia, and since she was sober, she couldn't take any of the pills that she used to abuse in the past. Ambien was one of those pills she couldn't have, so she stayed up most of the night, tossing and turning.

"What's the matter? Is it the baby?"

"No, he's fine. Jah was shot, and I need to head to the hospital."

I watched as she ripped the covers off her body as I did a few minutes ago and followed behind me back to my bedroom. "Calm down, Tweet. I need you to breathe because I know how you are."

"I'm really trying, Ma." I sighed and plopped down on the ottoman in front of the bed. "I just spoke to him, and he said he was coming home." I held my hand out and saw how terrified I was. My hands were shaking, and if Uzi wasn't sending a driver to pick me up, I wasn't sure if I would be able to drive myself to the hospital.

"Are you driving?"

"No, Uzi's sending a driver to me," I replied and went to pull on some clothes. I found some leggings, a white T-shirt, and pulled on a pair of sneakers.

When Paisley told me what the hell really happened to him, I felt like shit. I should have believed him when he told me that he was drugged. The truth was he had been drugged, and all this time that little bitch was extorting money out of him and making him believe that the baby was his. Our marriage went through hell all because a bitch wanted what we had. He begged me, and I continued to shut him out and ignore the hell out of him. In reality, I should have believed my husband and stuck by his side. Evelyn walked back into the room and picked up Taz.

"The driver is here and waiting. You call me and tell me everything when you get the chance. Taz will be fine," she informed me and kissed me on the cheek. "Breathe," she reminded me.

I let out a loud sigh, grabbed my purse, and headed to the car. It wasn't our usual driver, but he would just have to do for now. "Good morning, Mrs. McKnight," he greeted me. It had to be at least four or five in the morning. I got into the back of the Tahoe and waited for him to pull off.

For so long, I wanted a man to love the hell out of me. Then Jah came into my life, and he made everything alright for me. He showed me the love I needed and craved, and he made me his wife. I didn't have to force him to marry me; he wanted to do that. Not once did I ever have to question if this man's intentions were pure, because they were. Whenever I stared into his eyes, I could see the love he had for me. Jahquel had his flaws, and he lied like hell about the situation about his kids, but did that make him a bad person? He just cared too much and got caught up in the wrong things at the time. I said a silent prayer and sat back and waited until I arrived at the hospital.

Uzi and Remi were waiting downstairs for me when I arrived at the hospital. They rushed me upstairs to the waiting area and briefed me on what had happened. When Uzi mentioned that he was shot in the head, my knees grew weak. Remi quickly sat me down and held my hands. The doctors still hadn't come out and updated us on anything and I was worried. He couldn't leave me to raise this baby alone. We were supposed to grow old together, have more babies, and work on our marriage. Things weren't supposed to end like this, and I felt vomit tickle the back of my throat.

"I think I'm going to be sick." I gagged, stood up, and ran

to the bathroom down the hall. I didn't make it to a toilet and let the shrimp scampi I had for dinner last night come up all over the tiled floors. I continued to vomit until I was dry heaving. I felt so sick that I couldn't breathe. Why was this happening to me? What did I do to deserve all of the things that had been happening to me?

"Come on, sissy. Let me clean you up." Remi was right behind me and guided me over to the sink. I sat there like a baby as she wiped my face clean and spoke to me. If you offered to pay me six million dollars to tell you what she said, I wouldn't be able to answer or tell you.

All I knew was that my heart was broken in half. I needed to see Jah and make sure he was fine. Jahquel wouldn't leave me or his son. He couldn't leave us to fend for ourselves. He was the man of the house and had to be there. Our son had so many firsts that he had to be there to experience. Too many people depended on and loved Jah for him to leave us down here.

"Do you hear me, Tweet?" Remi touched my face and stared into my eyes. I could see the fear in her eyes too. She was trying to be there for both me and Uzi, but she was scared too.

"What?"

"He's going to be fine, Tweet. Jah wouldn't leave us, God isn't done with him yet," she told me, and I wanted to believe her so bad.

I wanted to believe that God wouldn't take him away from me, but I also knew that Jah had done a lot of shit. Karma was coming back to collect what was due to her, and he could die on me. These were thoughts that I didn't want to think, but I couldn't be so naïve to believe that I couldn't lose him. I wanted for this to be a dream and for me to wake up next to him and our son. Over these past few months, so much had been done and said, and I wished like hell I could take it all back. I told the man I vowed to love that I hated him. It was stuff like that, that made me feel like I was going to lose the love of my life. I had been so evil to him and said shit that I didn't mean just to hurt him, and now I was hurting like hell because of it.

Me and Remi went to sit back down in the waiting room where Uzi was sitting in the corner alone. His face screamed murder, and I knew he was about to turn the city upside down to find out whoever could have done this to Jah. Paris was cuddled up on the bench asleep, and me and Remi stayed cuddled in the other corner. I was glad to have my big sister here when I needed her. She could be asleep in bed while waiting on the news of Jah's outcome to come via phone. Instead, she was here with me and trying to console me. I closed my eyes and prayed that my husband was alive or at least fighting for his life. I couldn't lose him, I just couldn't.

It was four in the afternoon when they finally came out from surgery and updated us. The Arabic doctor was the first to come out. Both me and Uzi jumped up and walked over to him, desperate to hear any news from him.

"I'm assuming you're the family for Jahquel McKnight." He looked over his chart. I could tell it had been a long day for him. He had bags under his eyes, his hair was disheveled, and the way he walked from the back, I could tell he was tired.

"Yes, I'm his wife, and this is his brother," I anxiously replied.

"Is he dead, yes or no?" Uzi cut right to the chase. He didn't want to know anything except was his brother alive or dead.

"He's in critical condition. The bullet was successfully removed from his brain; however, we're not sure how much of if it caused damage to his brain. We won't be able to tell until he is awake."

"So he'll wake up?" This doctor just gave me more hope than he knew. "He'll wake up and be fine?"

The doctor sighed. "Mr. and Mrs. McKnight, I'm going to give it to you straight. We spent hours in that operating room, and he coded three times. Thankfully, we were able to bring him back. However, he had a bullet lodged in his brain, a bullet in his leg that traveled, but we were able to remove it, then another bullet hit his abdomen and obstructed his bowel, so we had to perform a partial colostomy. It's very touch and go right now, but we're hopeful that he'll pull through. While he's in this coma, we're going to be sure to continue to do tests to make sure everything is functioning as it should."

"Doc, he was able to walk some. Will he be able to walk again?"

"I can't tell you that. The longer he's bed ridden, the more his muscles will break down, so more than likely, he will be learning to do all those things again, should he wake up."

I couldn't hold it anymore and broke down. Hearing all that he had just told us just broke my entire heart. Who could be so heartless to do something like this to him? Jah didn't have any beef that I knew of, so who wanted him dead that bad? The bullet to the head was enough, but to continue to shoot him meant they wanted this man dead.

"He's still being hooked up to everything in CCU. Once he's done, you'll be able to go to in and see him. You're family, so there's no visitor's hours for you guys." He touched my hand. "Again, I'm sorry we had to meet under these circumstances." He fished in his pocket and handed me a card. "While he's here, I'll be the main doctor on his case. My personal and work cell is on there; don't hesitate to give me a call if you need me."

"Thank you, Doctor."

The CCU unit was all the way on the west wing and you

had to be buzzed into the unit. The lights were dimmed, and there were a bunch of rooms with different patients in the room. Tubes, wires, and everything else hung from each patient's body. The nurse was sitting at the station reading a book and occasionally looking at the computer monitor. When she noticed us come in, she closed her kindle cover and averted her attention to the both of us.

"You're here for the new transfer?" she assumed. I guess they didn't get too many visitors back here. From the three rooms and the one in the back, I could tell she knew every and anybody who walked through those doors after she buzzed them in.

"Yes. Where is he?" I just needed to lay eyes on my husband. Even when I did finally lay my eyes on him, I knew it still wouldn't be good. I wouldn't walk in on my sarcastic husband who always had a reply for everything.

"He's in the room to the back. Make sure you both sign in here, and there's no visitor's hours here," she informed us. "Food is allowed in the room, and no more than two people are allowed in here at one time," she continued.

"How do we go about getting him a private room?"

"I get asked this question almost daily. The doctors want him where they need him. The operation room is only two floors down from where we are. That's approximately three minutes to get down there in case of a complication. This unit was strategically placed here for that reason. Until he's up, out the woods and talking, he'll be in this until."

"How much do I need to break you off to bring in more than two people?"

"Break me off?" She scoffed with disgust.

"Yeah. How much can I pay you to look the other way?" Money was the motive and everyone always had a price. If Uzi had to pay her a grand per person, he would do it, and she would take the money.

"Sir, you can't just bribe me to bring more people up here. Your family member is down there." She pointed and plopped back down in her chair.

"Bet," he said and left a hundred-dollar bill on top of the desk. We walked away, and I turned my head and just like we both knew, she stuffed it into her bra and opened that kindle case back up to read.

When I entered the room, my knees buckled at the sight of Jah. He had so many tubes attached to him that if I wanted to hug him, I couldn't. there were tubes coming from his head, mouth, chest, and everywhere imaginable. Machines were labeled with alphabets, and there were at least six fluid bags hanging from each machine. Some were clear or yellow. My heart was at the pit of my stomach, staring at the man I loved. The machine was currently breathing for him, and every couple seconds, his chest would heave up and down with a sound from the machine. Uzi was staring at his brother, and a tear escaped his eye as he walked closer. I put my hand on his, and it was ice cold. There was no sign that his body had any warmth to it, and it made me cry harder than I already was.

"I want whoever did this to him dead." I sobbed as I sat in the chair next to his bed. Who could be this cruel to him? I had to sit back and remember that Jah lived the street life and there wasn't any loyalty when it came to the streets.

"Sis, you ain't said shit but a word. I'm gonna handle that shit soon as I leave here," he promised me and kissed me on the forehead. Then he went over to the opposite side of Jah and bent down in his tube covered face. "Bro, I'm gonna get at those niggas. Rest up, because we need you, man." His voice cracked.

"Who the fuck would do him like this? Why was he even alone?" I wondered out loud.

Since I'd known Jah, he had always been so careful. He

was rarely alone when he couldn't walk, but now that he got around with his walker, he liked to be alone. I understood why. He had gained his independence back and now wanted to use it. Like hell I wished he was watching his surroundings because this would have prevented us from being in this situation. I just wanted to crawl on the floor and die from the way I felt. I was so worn down from everything we had been going through. Our marriage was in the toilet, I was forced to be a single mother, and now when it seemed like we could work things out, this happened. I knew God gave battles to his strongest warriors, yet I was tired and didn't want to fight anymore. I just wanted to toss my hands up and surrender. How much more could he hand over my way? I'd always saw myself as being strong and could get through anything. Right now, I wanted to give up and stop fighting. What was the point?

Remi knocked on the door, and both me and Uzi looked her way. "The nurse came and got me and allowed Paris to sleep in one of the empty rooms. I can't believe this." She walked closer to Jah's bed. "We need to find out who did this and handle them."

"Calm down, YG. I'll handle this and figure out who is at the bottom of this. I just sent a message out to Manic and Grizz; they should be on their way now."

"Parrish, you need to be careful. If someone did this to Jah, this isn't an accident. I want you to promise me that yo—"

"Baby, I don't want to hear none of that shit. If I gotta die while trying to get the nigga that did this to my brother, then so be it."

"You're selfish, Parrish. Are me and Paris not even a thought? What about us?"

"What the fuck do you mean, what about us? Remi, my damn husband is laid up in here on his death bed, and you're worried about yourself? When you were shot, did you give him the same speech, or were you right there to kill the nigga who tried to end your life? Jahquel is his fucking brother, and if this man wants to paint the city red and die while doing it, then that's what the fuck he'll do!" I hollered at my older sister.

Remi had some fucking nerve pulling that selfish shit in the middle of all of this. How dare she sit up here and make this all about her. Everyone always mentioned how selfish Remi was, and I never complained or saw it. However, right here and now, the way she was acting, I could see right through her.

"Tweeti, we have a baby on the wa—"

"Get the fuck out of the room. All of you!" I raised my voice again and looked at both she and Uzi. He didn't do anything, but he needed to leave because I needed a minute to myself.

"Time the fuck out." Uzi held his hand up toward me. "You're pregnant?"

Remi had tears coming down her face. "I found out last week and was waiting for the right time to tell you. You need to be here for me, Paris, and our baby," she told him.

"Are you fucking serious? Get the fuck out of this room before I go the fuck off. My damn husband is laying in here fighting for his life, and you're discussing your future? My son may not have a damn father when it's all said and done."

Remi tried to come over to me, and I held my hand up. "I'm sorry, Tweeti. I jus—"

"Babe, just go right now... I'll meet you home," Uzi told Remi. "I get you're going through it, but what I'm not going to do is leave my brother. I don't give a fuck what I say or do, this my blood, and I'm not going no damn where." He switched his attention over to me.

This was what pissed me off about Uzi. He never knew

when the fuck to back the fuck up and let me handle shit. Whenever something happened to his siblings, he basically disregarded that they had spouses. He did the same thing with Wynner until she cut him out of her marriage. If she didn't, Qua, her husband, would come second to her damn brother.

"No, you will leave with your fiancée, and when I'm ready to have you both come up here, I'll call. What we're not about to do is push me to the side like I'm not this man's wife. You're his brother. Once he slipped this ring on my finger, I became the bitch that signs. Remember what Kash Doll said?"

"Why the fuck would I know what Kash Doll said?" he barked. I could tell he was pissed at me about what I was saying.

"Everything got my name on it; ring finger got his ring on it." I flashed my wedding ring.

"Yo, she playing hella games right now like I won't have her thrown the fuck out this hospital."

"Nurse!" I yelled.

She slammed closed her Kindle and came right over to where we were. "I need you to have them taken out of this room. I want to approve anybody who wants to visit."

"Sir, can you please leave," the nurse spoke to Uzi, and he looked like he wanted to box her in the mouth.

"Get the fuck out—"

"Babe, she wants us gone, so we need to respect that. Tweet, I'm so sorry, and I didn't mean to make it about us. When you're ready for us to come back up, we will. Can you please keep us updated?"

"Yeah," was all I said. Remi was able to calm Uzi down, and he left while mumbling shit under his breath.

Me and Uzi never had the perfect relationship. He was used to everyone bowing down to him, and I wasn't about to do that. No one hardly challenged what Uzi had to say, and that wasn't me. I always had something to say, and it was why we budded heads. The reason me and him hadn't budded heads in a while was because we were never really around each other. He was busy planning his wedding, and I was dealing with my son, husband that cheated on me, and moving into a new home. With Jah in his current condition, Uzi wasn't about to storm in here like this was his show. I was the bitch running shit, and I was going to make the decisions that would lead to hopefully saving my husband's life.

❧ 3 ❧

PAISLEY

"**W**hat you mean she's not letting anyone up there to see him?" Manic paced back and forth butt ass naked.

Manic didn't like towel drying; he preferred to air dry while walking around the house naked. Eating a bowl of cereal while this man walked around naked with his dick swinging around wasn't what I pictured seeing this afternoon. This pregnancy was draining the hell out of me, and I felt like I had no energy to do anything. All I did was sleep, eat, and watch movies. Me and Manic had been staying at separate apartments. I just wanted him to have his space, and I wanted to have my own space as well. For years, I shared an apartment with a man, and I had actually come to love my own place and space. It felt nice going grocery shopping and buying things that I actually liked to eat. For once, I was getting to know myself, and it felt nice. Mitchell wasn't weird about it and respected the space I needed.

"What happened?" I asked with a mouth full of cereal. Clearly, something happened, and he was pissed because he kept mumbling obscenities under his breath.

"Jah got shot, and he's in a coma. Tweeti isn't letting anybody up there right now." He tossed his phone on the couch beside him.

"Oh my word. Are you serious?"

"Babe, what the fuck you think? You think I'm turning red and shit for fun?" he barked, which was unusual for him.

"Let me call her. She probably needs some food or just company." I jumped off the stool and went into the bedroom for my phone.

"If she allows you up there, let me come with you." Manic came into the bedroom right behind me.

"Nope. If she's not allowing you guys up there, it may be for a reason. Not to mention, you being a smart ass in the kitchen is another reason why the fuck I wouldn't bring you with me." I touched Tweeti's name on my phone and put the phone to my ear.

"C'mon, I was fucking playing." He tried to cop a plea like his ass wasn't being a smart ass a few seconds ago.

"Hey, Tweet. I heard what happened. Can I come bring you anything?" I put the phone on speaker while I grabbed some clothes to put on.

"Yeah, I'm just trying to take it one day at a time. In fact, it's only been two days, and I'm about to pull my hair out."

"I'm so sorry you're going through this. I'll stop and grab some coffee and some food. Where's Taz? Is he okay?"

"Girl, I really appreciate that. I haven't left his side and have been eating this nasty ass hospital food. He's good. He misses me and his father, but he's home with my mother."

"I can grab you some things from your house before heading to you."

"Paisley, if you could, I would appreciate that so much. I'll have my mother get me a bag together so all you have to do is grab the bag."

"Okay, sounds good. See you in a bit," I told her and ended the call.

Manic was pulling on underwear and grabbing a pair of sweatpants. "You gonna need a ride or else you plan on buying a metro card."

"I swear you're so petty. If you don't drive me to Staten Island and then back to this hospital, I won't let you see your baby being born."

"Nah, you wouldn't," he challenged me.

"Try me." I smirked as I snapped my bra on. "I'll tell them that I don't want anyone in the room, and you know mother's word takes priority when you're in the hospital. Is this a risk you want to take, Mitchell?" I walked over to him and hugged him around the waist.

Mitchell looked down at me and kissed me on the lips. "Why you got to play hard ball? You know I want to see my baby come into this world."

"Let me put some deodorant on and then we can go." I smirked and went into the bathroom.

It was so different getting my way with Mitchell. I could tell him I wanted the world, and he would try and get it for me. With Rome, I had to bow down to him and do what he wanted. Rome wanted everything about him, and I came somewhere down the line. With Mitchell, I could throw a tantrum, and he would try every way to make it work for me. If I pulled that shit with Rome, he would beat the shit out of me and make me apologize to him for throwing a tantrum in the first place. Things were different, and every morning when I opened my eyes, I had to pinch myself. I couldn't believe I was living the life that I was living. When my feet touched the wooden floors in the morning, I didn't have to worry about catching a train to work and working all day. I never had to worry about getting home before Rome to make sure dinner was on the table.

"Nisha, I hear you. I'll be there tomorrow." I came out the bathroom to Mitchell on the phone.

All I could do was roll my eyes. I was trying so hard to be the bigger person in this situation, but the further along we both got, the more harder it became. She was further along than me, and I felt like she was always calling Mitchell to do some outlandish shit. The kicker was that his dumb ass always went and ended up doing it. I was tired of her, and she hadn't even had the baby yet.

"What she called for?" I jumped on him soon as he ended the call with Nisha. What could she possibly need? This woman had more needs than me, and I was a high-risk pregnancy. All I required was food, sleep, and rides to my appointments every so often.

"We got an appointment tomorrow, and she was calling me to remind me." He slipped his feet into a pair of slides.

"Which appointment is this for?"

"She made one at this 3D shit. We gotta pay out of pocket because she wants to see the baby in 3D."

"Did her doctor tell her to do this, or is she just doing this because she wants to?"

"Paisl—"

"No, I want to know." I cut him off. He was always telling everyone else no, but for some reason, he couldn't tell Nisha that he didn't want to come. "Correct me if I'm wrong, but she already has a 3D sonogram from your last appointment, am I right?"

"Yeah, bu—"

"Why the fuck do you need to be there for this one? Y'all just went two weeks ago, and you got that one, so ain't shit changed that much with the baby in two weeks." Nisha knew what she was doing. She was making all these appointments so he could go with her.

"I won't go," he finally gave in and told me.

"You're right. You won't be going, because this is ridiculous. I understand she's having your baby, but damn, Mitchell. You expect me to put up with this shit our entire pregnancy?"

"Nah, you right, and if the shoe was on the other foot, I would be complaining too."

"Now I'm complaining? All I'm doing is pointing out the obvious. She's using these little outings to spend time with you. How could you be so blind to what she's doing?"

He shook his head. "Stop getting all worked up with my baby in your stomach. You don't need to be stressing. I said I wouldn't go, so end the shit."

"On second thought, I really don't need you to drive me anywhere. I'd rather get around alone today." I whipped out my phone and ordered me an Uber. His entire attitude with this Nisha shit had me already in my feelings. He was the first person to call someone out on their shit, and he had yet to do that with Nisha. She always had these appointments, and it was all skeptical. I was a high-risk pregnancy, and I had maybe two appointments a month. From what Manic told me, her pregnancy was developing normal, and there were no complications.

"You dead ass, Paisley?"

"Yep. You can go and do whatever you need to do with Nisha for the day. I've been put last for a bunch of years, and I refuse to be put last again. If she is who comes first, then I will put me and this baby first."

"She's carrying my baby."

"And I'm carrying your baby. Not only am I carrying your baby, I'm your girlfriend. Or is that still up in the air too?"

"You know it's not. Why you tripping?"

"Bye... lock up when you're done, and I'll see you later." I grabbed my purse and headed out the door.

This was why we kept two separate apartments. When I needed a break, I was able to have my own place and didn't have to look him in the face. Like now, I needed a few days to myself because I was sick of this Nisha shit that kept coming up. I was tired of him constantly answering the call when we were laying together or running out because he forgot an appointment. It seemed like I was constantly telling him that it was fine because all he did was apologize about shit. She was carrying his baby, and I understood all of that. Still, where did I fit into any of this? It seemed like he was more active in her pregnancy than he was with mine. Maybe I was jealous or even a little insecure. How could I not be? Nisha was beautiful, and she had her life together. She didn't need Manic for a damn thing. Not to mention, she admitted that she was in love with him, so how was I supposed to take them spending time together? What if one time he decides to take things further than the appointment? Where did that leave me? It never dawned on me that Manic could do his own thing and that would leave me heartbroken.

It didn't take me long to head to Staten Island and back to the hospital where Tweet was. When I walked into the room, it was dark except for the TV and the lights on the machines. Jah was hooked up to so many machines I didn't know where to start with counting. Tweeti was laid on the sofa in the room, and I gently tapped her.

"Ma'am, how did you get in here?" A nurse happened to be walking by and peeked in the room. "There's no visitors, and any visitors have to be approved by his wife."

"She's fine." Tweeti stirred from her sleep and began stretching. "Thank you, Ronda." She thanked the nurse and sat up.

"It's like Fort Dix up in here," I joked to lighten the mood. "How are you?" I sat down where her feet were once at.

"Drained, tired, and worried. I haven't seen my baby in two days, but I don't want to leave his side. My mama has been trying to get up here, but they don't allow babies up in here."

"I'm sorry. What happened?"

"All we know is that he was shot. I can't tell you anything else because I don't know. He was shot in the head like some damn animal."

"The head?" I gasped. "Tweet, I'm so sor—"

She held her hand up. "Stop apologizing. You didn't do it, and you can't heal him, so apologizing does nothing for me."

"S... Where's his family? Did they come up?"

"They came up here this morning. Evelyn does more harm than good. All she does is complain and blame everyone. I'm already stressed, and I don't need any more."

"Understandable. Let me take you to grab some food or something."

"No, I can't leave this room. I need to be here if he wakes up."

"When."

"Huh?"

"You said *if* and I said *when*. Jah is strong and will wake up. We need to speak that into the universe so it can come right back to us."

"You're right," she replied as she stared into space. "Thank you. You really didn't have to do all of this, but you did, and I appreciate it."

"Of course. I tried calling Sundae on the way to your house to see if she wanted to ride with me back."

"Girl, Sundae got drama up to her ass." She whistled and put me on to all that had been happening with Sundae.

When she told me everything that was going on, I gasped. I couldn't believe that she had been taking sugar pills all this damn time. In Miami, she stared at me with fear in her eyes because she didn't know what was going on with her own body. I remembered her going through it and telling me that she didn't feel like herself and was scared. To hear that someone tried to sabotage her was really sad. Since I'd met Sundae, she had always been open and honest about her mental illness, and since I'd met her, I'd witness her take it seriously. Especially when she felt like her and Grizz were getting to a place where he stopped seeing her as a patient, and he stopped being a care giver.

"I feel so sorry for her. That must have felt like torture, not knowing what is going on with your own body."

"Yeah, I feel for her. She was supposed to be discharged, and I called her yesterday, but I know she's in her feelings and will hit me back when she wants to talk."

"She's going back to that house?"

"Honestly? I don't know. I told her she could have stayed with me. Sundae is super independent, and when she's hurt, she tends to push people away. I wish I could be there for her, but I have to deal with this and can't be at two places at once. Shit, three places, because my baby needs me too."

"I'm home all day anyway. I can make sure that Sundae is fine," I promised her. "You worry about Jah and being there *when* he wakes up."

"Thank you, Paisley. What is going on with you?"

"No, I don't need to bog you down with my stupid problems."

Tweeti went and grabbed her water from the table and sat back down beside me. "It'll be a nice escape from here. Tell me what's going on?"

I broke down and told her everything with Manic and Nisha. Hell, I even told her my own insecurities I held about Manic cheating on me because I depended on him. Tweeti listened and didn't pass judgement on me. It felt nice to just have someone listen while I spilled my thoughts, incomplete thoughts, and rants out at them. When I was done, she passed me her water bottle, and I guzzled the cold water.

"That bitch is in love with your man. You have every reason to feel how you do," she started. "Next, you also need to check your feelings when it comes to him and this baby. You're salty that you're not the only one pregnant, and I can see it when you speak about her pregnancy."

"This was supposed to be a special moment for the both of us. We're supposed to both be having our first child together, and now it's ruined because Nisha wants to turn up pregnant."

"That may be true, but you had to remember this man has to split his time between two pregnant women who will be hormonal. Her excessive doctor appointments are a bit much, and he needs to get in her ass about that. The more you force that man to choose, he will choose his kids, and there goes your chance at being happy with the man you want to be with. Stop making him feel like he has to pick between spending time with you or going to see his baby on the monitor at some overpriced sonogram center."

"Are those places really that expensive?"

"Yes, and insurance don't cover them. I was obsessed with seeing my baby, so I went twice a week," she admitted and laughed. "Jah loved seeing them when he got home from working. I understand why she's going, but he doesn't need to be there for every sonogram appointment, especially if it's not her doctor's office."

"Thank you, Tweet." I smiled.

"Don't mention it."

❧ 4 ❧

SUNDAE

W hen I opened my eyes, all I wanted to do was close them again. The bright sun from the curtains were blaring right into my face. Shifting my body, I was able to block the sun from my face and close my eyes again. I didn't expect to be back home with my mama. This was the last place I wanted to be, yet here I was laying in my twin size bed. The springs in the bed creaked as I tried to get comfortable in this uncomfortable ass bed. This room had such terrible memories for me. On the wall near the small closet was a blood stain from when I tried to slit my wrist in seventh grade. My mother rushed into my room and caught me just in time and pulled the razor out my hands. Over near the wooden dresser that had seen better days, was a cigarette burn. I remember smoking a carton of cigarettes and then taking the last one and burning the inside of my thighs. For years, I didn't want to live. All I wanted to do was die and be sent up to God to rest peacefully. Stress was brought on by my manic behaviors, and it was what caused me not to take my medicine. The last time I was admitted into the crazy house, I promised myself that I would be and do better.

Teyanna fucked around with my medicine, and I wasn't myself, and Grizz didn't notice. It hurt me that he chose to continue to protect and stick up for this woman instead of me. I told him something wasn't right with her, and he continued to place blame on me like I was the one who was causing trouble. Since the day Teyanna stepped foot into our home, she didn't like me and had a vendetta against me. She knew what she was going to do to me before she stepped over the threshold of our home. That bitch aimed to ruin my entire life, and Grizz helped her do it. He should have known me better and knew that what I was feeling was real. Instead, he continued to accuse, belittle, and ignore my feelings like I was some bitch he had just met off the streets. What made all of this sad was that he did this to me over an ex-girlfriend. If the knife wasn't already in my back, he had pushed it so far that it came out of my chest.

"Wake ya crazy ass on up. You not gonna be sleeping all day around here." My mother rushed into the room with a baby on her hip.

My mother ran a daycare out of her apartment and collected decent money. The thing was, she had a terrible gambling problem. She and Evelyn used to throw card parties back in the day. My mother went from throwing card parties to spending all her damn money in the casinos. You could find her there every weekend, and if she got some extra money, she would be there during the week too.

"I wish you stop saying shit like that," I grumbled and pulled the covers over my head. "And change that baby's diaper; it smells like shit."

"Don't be in here telling me what the fuck I need to do with this baby. You better get up and help me with these damn kids. Lashonda came and brought her twins, and I need some help."

"Not my problem. I'm supposed to be resting." I reached my hand out the cover and grabbed my cell phone that was vibrating on the chair beside the bed.

"Like hell it is. You think you gonna be laying around here, eating up this food, and not going to put no work in? Hell nah. You got the game all fucked up, Sundae."

"Hey, what's going on?" I answered the phone and ignored my mother. If she knew what was good with her, she better had left me alone. I gave her six hundred dollars to pay her rent this month so I could stay here without hearing her mouth.

"Hey, Sundae. I heard what's going on with you and wanted to check on you," Paisley replied. It was nice that she called to check on me; it meant a lot to me.

"Sundae, get your ass up, and don't make me have to come back."

"I'm not getting up to do shit. The doctors want me to rest, and that six hundred dollars I paid your ass says the same thing. Give my damn money back, and I'll help you." When I said that, she got quiet. This was going to be temporary. I could feel myself being stressed, and I hadn't even been here a week.

"Sundae?"

"Yeah, I'm sorry, girl. I'm back at my mama's house, and she's driving me fucking crazy." I sat up on the side of the bed and kicked my feet.

I would have rather been anywhere else except here with my mama. Hotels were too expensive, and even if I stayed a week, I would have ended up here after. Grizz handed me money like it was going out of style. I would say I want to go shopping, and he would hand me thousands of dollars. Instead of spending it stupidly, I always put it in the bank for a rainy day. The day came when I needed to use my umbrella, and that was the money I planned to live off of.

"You're back with your mom? Why?"

"'Cause I refuse to go back to Grizz's stank ass house. I really need to get out of this house, man. It's not good for my mental."

"Are you okay, Sundae?"

"Yeah, I'm good. I've just realized that my mother is one of my triggers. This is why I avoided the hell out of her and don't have a relationship with her."

Paisley sighed on the other end of the line. "I'm sorry you're going through all of this. If you need somewhere to stay, I have an extra bedroom. I don't need to convert it to a nursery for quite some time, so you can stay here with me. I'm alone here most of the time, so I don't mind."

When it felt like the odds were stacked against me, Paisley came through. "Seriously? I mean, of course I plan on getting my own place, but that's not going to happen right now."

"I don't mind. I would actually like the company."

"Thank you, Paisley. You don't understand how much this means to me."

Nobody except for Grizz knew that I was pregnant. I had plans on telling Tweeti soon, but right now, I still had to process all of this. A baby was what I wanted, and both me and Grizz spoke about it. Still, I didn't think it would happen so soon, especially with all that was going on right now. This was supposed to be a joyous occasion, and now it felt like the worst news I could have heard. I wanted a baby by Grizz bad, and I wanted us to raise our baby together. Now, I had to make big decisions on what this meant for me. Was I mentally prepared to be a single mother?

"Sundae?" Paisley interrupted me from my thoughts. I had forgot she was even on the phone this entire time.

"Oh, I'm sorry. Can I bring my bags over today, or is that too soon?"

"Nope, that's fine. I would offer you a ride, but I don't have a car," she joked.

"I'm fine. I have my car." Thankfully, I was able to swing by the house and grab my car with the spare key I kept in my purse. Grizz wasn't home, and I was glad because I didn't want to hear his mouth or his excuses he had as to why I needed to come home. I'd never been so sure in my life that being away from him was the right decision I needed to make for me.

"Okay. I'll send you the address, and I'll let the doorman know that you're coming," she told me.

"Thank you, Paisley. I really appreciate you for doing this for me."

"Don't mention it, girl. See you soon." We ended the call, and I rushed around the room to gather all my things. My stuff wasn't spread all over the place, but I did have some clothes here and there. Paisley said she didn't mind, so I was about to leave this hell hole right now before I was in prison for strangling the hell out of my mother. My grumbling stomach caused me to stop dead in my track and plop down on the bed. I had a baby in my stomach, and I couldn't walk around and ignore the fact that this baby needed nourishment. Usually, I would have continued with my day, not bothering to fill my body with food. This baby didn't ask to be here, so I needed to make sure that I did all I could to assure I had a healthy baby.

"About time you dragged your ass out that bed. Now, I need you to run down to the corner store and get me some pampers and formula. That damn Rika gonna give me my damn money back," she mumbled as I poured myself a bowl of cereal. "How the hell she gonna bring her baby over here with no damn diapers or food?"

"I'm not going to the store," I let her know as I sat down at the kitchen table. "This isn't what I signed up for, you did. This is how you pay your bills, that's cool. However, you're not going to make me run here and there for you."

"Lil' gir—"

"I'm not a fucking little girl anymore. You will address me as a grown ass woman." My mother had always made me feel like a child, even while being an adult. I understood she was my mother, and I had to respect her, but I was tired of being treated like a damn little girl when I was a grown woman.

"Child, the way your crazy ass carry around here, you're a little girl. How many times I've been dragged out my bed because your crazy ass got into some shit?"

"I'm not staying here anymore." There was no need in arguing back and forth with her. I was tired of doing this shit with her, and she needed to know that I didn't need her.

"Where else you gonna go? That nigga of yours got tired of you, and where he at?"

Getting up from the table, I left my bowl of cereal there and went into the room to finish packing shit. My mother couldn't respect when someone needed their own personal space. If I left the kitchen, that meant I needed a minute. Instead, that meant she needed to follow me and continue to pick a fight with me.

"Mama, leave me alone."

"Hell nah. You better get in there and finish that cereal. My stamps are not about to be wasted. You better go ahead and handle that shit now."

I grabbed my Gucci duffle bag and slipped my feet into my slippers and walked right by her. "That baby's diaper smells horrible. Change that damn diaper!" I barked as I walked out the door and down the hallway of the building.

My mother stuck her head out the door and hollered, "Don't bring your stupid ass back over this way either!"

JAHQUEL J.

Holding back the tears, I continued out of the building and hit the locks to my car. After tossing my things in the back seat, I got behind the wheel and let all the tears roll down my cheeks. How could a mother speak to her only child like that? It was a shame how much hate my mother really had for me. I tried to understand what I had done to her that was so bad for her to treat me like this. My mental illness—I couldn't control. It wasn't something that I wanted to have; I was born with it. From what my grandmother told me, my great aunt had struggled with the same thing before she took her own life. My mother tried to keep my grandmother from speaking on it, and she continued anyway. I wanted to be on my medicine for my child and to be a better woman. I was done with running wild, being impulsive, and hurting the people I truly cared for. My doctor had found the right kind of medication that would continue to help me but wouldn't cause any harm for the baby. Wiping my tears, I started my car and pulled away from the building. If I had to sleep on the streets, I'd do it to avoid coming back to this place.

I RUSHED OFF THE ELEVATOR AND WAS BUZZED RIGHT INTO the CCU unit at the hospital. Tweeti had called me while I was on my way to Paisley's house, and I rushed right over here. I had no clue all of this was going on. Here I was in my own head, dealing with my own issues, and I didn't realize my best friend could possibly be a widow. When I entered the room, Tweeti looked up from the magazine she was reading. She looked so out of it, pale, and her hair was all over her head. She wore a pair of leggings, hospital socks, and a big T-shirt. When she noticed me, she abandoned the magazine and came and hugged me tightly.

"How are you? Are you alright? What's going on?" She bombarded me with question after question. I should have been the one asking her all the questions, not the other way around.

"I'm fine. This is not about me. How is Jah? I'm sorry. I would have gotten here sooner if I would have known."

"Don't worry about any of that. I know you were dealing with things. You're here now, and that's all that matters." She pulled me over to the couch and sat down next to me.

"What happened?"

"Someone shot him. We don't know who or why, but he was shot, and now we're here. The doctors haven't seen any improvement." She sighed.

"I'm sorry. I hate that you're going through this."

"Me too. I'm just so tired of things happening to us. When can we just chill and rest and not have shit happen to us?"

"I'm pregnant."

Tweeti looked at me through squinted eyes. "Seriously?" The only reason I blurted it out was because I could see her about to be emotional. She needed her mind to focus on something else, even if it was just for a couple minutes.

"Yeah. I found out when they admitted me into the hospital. I'm scared, Tweet."

"Why? You're an amazing aunt to Taz; you'll be an amazing mama too." She hugged me and kissed me on the cheek.

"That's different. I don't have to care for Taz. He has two parents that do that. All I provide is toys and kisses. This baby will depend on me entirely, and I'm not sure if I'm up to the job."

"Sund—"

"No, Tweeti. Listen to me. You know my past and what I'm capable of. What if that happens again and I have a baby? I'm already weak mentally, and first-time mothers go through all types of things. What if I can't handle it? I'm going to be a single mother too."

Tweeti grabbed my hand and stared me in the eyes. "I'm here. I know in the past I wasn't there, and I should have been, but you're not doing this alone. You have me, Evelyn, and everyone else who loves you. Not to mention, you have Grizz, and he's not going to turn his back on you or that baby."

"Fuck him," I mumbled.

"Right now, you're in your feelings about him, which you have every right to be. We don't know what the hell was going through Grizz's head when he did that dumb shit, but we know he's a good man, and he'll be a good father." She looked toward the door and saw Emory walk in.

"I spoke to the doctor, and we're going to move him," she announced without even greeting neither of us. I didn't expect me, but damn, she could have greeted Tweeti.

"No, you're not. The doctor that has been on his case has been very helpful, and I don't want to switch hospitals."

"Child, I know what's best for my son. And I will do what's *best* for my son. There's a hospital in Jersey that me and Shad's friend works at. He's the best in the country, and I know he'll be able to provide more care than this place." She looked around the room disgusted.

"Do you know how much strain and toll that will put on his body? Have the doctor come here and ask for privileges to treat Jah here. If not, then I'm not signing off on that." Tweeti went by Jah's side and kissed his hand. "I'm not going to move him because of what you think is best for him."

"You do know I was being nice by even telling you? It's already being processed." She walked on the opposite side of Jah and touched his other hand.

Tweeti pressed the nurse button, and a nurse damn near broke her neck to get into the room. "Yes, Mrs. McKnight?"

"I want to speak to the chief of the hospital and the attending doctor this afternoon," Tweeti told her, and she nodded.

"I'll page both of them and let them know. Is there anything else I can get you?"

"No, that'll be all."

"Emory, I don't know who died and made you in charge of things here, and I don't know who the hell you spoke to, but I make the decisions when it comes to this man. Yeah, you've made the decision to get him circumcised so he could grow up and deliver miraculous dick, but I'm his wife, and you're not going to continue to waltz around here like me or my decisions don't matter. I'm his wife, and you're his mother." Tweeti didn't raise her voice, yell, or even use her hands to speak. Instead, she massaged her husband's hands while staring Emory right in the eye.

"Tweeti, he wouldn't even be in this mess if it wasn't for you and your dramatics. He made a mistake, and you kick him out the home our family's money bought. You got your crackhead mama living up in there seeing my grandson more than I see him."

"Oh hell..." I allowed my voice to trail off because Tweeti held her hand up. Emory had some damn nerve to walk up in there talking shit and then to mention her mother when everyone knew that was a sore subject for her.

"When a dog makes a mess in their home, you put them out the house. Maybe you never learned that, but I'm a woman that is raising a little boy who thinks the world of me. I refuse to be looked at as less then because I allowed his father to walk all over me because he has a big bank account. You slap a dog on the nose, and they'll learn their mistake. Your son here learned his mistake. He learned that I'm not the type of bitch that's going to sit back and allow him to collect kids like a damn China Cabinet. I don't care how much money, what kind of car I drive, or where I live, I will not tolerate disrespect. You think he's out the dog house because he's shot? Hell nah, that nigga still has work to do, because he still fucking lied." She raised her voice a bit.

"Mrs. McKnight?"

"Yes," both Emory and Tweeti answered in unison.

"Oh, I didn't realize... Well, the one that's married to Jahquel McKnight." The doctor chuckled. "I'm Cory Ram, the chief of this hospital. Again, I'm so sorry for what has happened. We've been keeping the police and media away from the hospital. Your husband is in no shape to answer any questions." He shook Tweeti's hand.

"Thank you, Mr. Ram. I really appreciate that. I'm trying to figure out what's going on with moving my husband."

"Ah, yes. We're arranging transport right now. I know you wanted it done as quick as possible, but this takes time but we're wo—"

"I never asked to have my husband moved. His mother, the other Mrs. McKnight, has requested that." Tweeti cut him off.

"Oh, I'm so sorry. When we received the call, she only mentioned her last name, so we assumed it was you. We're so sorry for this mishap, and it won't happen again." He quickly apologized.

"I want my son moved out of this hospital immediately. I'm his mother."

"You're not his next of kin, which is his wife. Whatever she says goes. We have to do what his wife wants and request, so I'm sorry. If you need me, have one the nurses page me."

"Thank you," Tweeti replied and came to sit back down on the couch. "If you would like to leave, Emory, you can. The only reason I haven't banned you from coming up here is because this is your son. Don't get it twisted. I will."

"Keeping my kids away from their brother during this time is disgusting."

"No, I'm keeping your grown ass man away from his brother. Wynner can't seem to get away from being a mother and wife to see her brother. If she did, she would know she's allowed to come up here," she corrected her.

Emory didn't have anything else to say, so she left the room. We could hear her heels clacking as she made it down the hallway. The nerve this lady had to come and try to call the shots like she was in charge.

"How do you put up with that bitch?"

"I don't. Emory cares about Emory. And she has made it clear plenty of times that when it's all said and done, that I'm just Jah's wife, and I shouldn't have as much opinion as I do."

"I would be in someone's jail."

"She's not worth it. I know if she mentions my mother one more time, I'm gonna beat her ass. She better stop mentioning my damn family like her family is so perfect. She got a daughter who puts herself last, and her kids and husband come first. A son who hid his daughter from his family for years and has an issue with a woman taking lead, and Jah who has so many damn issues that I don't have one to directly point out. Then, she has her husband who is so unhappy with her but stays because he can't afford to embarrass her again. Last time she walked away with half, and he was able to make that back, but this time, she'll go for more, and they're not even legally married."

"Misery loves company, and that's why she's coming up here bothering you."

"Girl, she has nothing better to do. Remi told me a few months ago she and Uzi saw Shad out with another woman. When he saw them, he came over to their table and introduced ole girl as his business partner for that chain of smoothie stores they just opened. When they went back over to their table and Uzi was paying their bill, she saw Shad kiss that woman on the lips."

"She told Emory?"

"Hell no. She would just make her out to be the liar. Remi said she's not getting in any of their business and hasn't spoke on it since."

"I kind of feel bad for her."

"Don't. She doesn't even feel bad for her own self. Anyway, I appreciate you being here, I really do."

"Of course." I smiled at her. "I'm going to be staying with Paisley."

"Why you choose there and not my house?"

"Because you're too close. I don't want to be too close to Grizz. He'll be down at your place every day, and I really just need time away from him.

"I understand." She sighed. "I'm here all day and everyday anyway."

"You need to get some air, Tweet. Come with me to Paisley's house," I told her. She needed to get out and get refreshed.

"No, I'm staying here. I'd appreciate if you go and get me soul food from up the block." She giggled.

"You lucky I love you." I smiled. I chatted with Tweeti for a bit then went to get her some food before leaving to head to Paisley's place. She told me she just got home, and I was free to come over anytime I would like. It felt nice to finally have a place to lay my head down without hearing someone call me a crazy bitch or demand that I do something for them. In reality, all I wanted to do was be at home in bed with Grizz, but life didn't work out that way.

5

GRIZZ

A nigga hadn't been home, and I was missing my baby. When I went up to the hospital, she had already been discharged, and they refused to give me any information on what was going on with her. Then I went home in hopes of catching up and realized that she had taken her car and grabbed some clothes too. Her phone was going to voicemail, and I could only assume that she had blocked me from getting in touch with her. If none of that was worse, then I had to learn that Jah had got caught slipping and someone tried to body him. Hearing that my nigga was fighting for his life and there wasn't a damn thing I could do about it, I was pissed. I was mad as fuck that this shit happened to him. The thing that kept going through my mind was who would want to body him that bad? I mean, there were a bunch of niggas that was bitten by the envy bug; however, none of them were bold enough to touch Uzi or Jah. They knew what would happen to them if shit went left.

"Anybody heard anything?" Uzi questioned and took a pull from his blunt. My nigga stopped smoking a while back, and the stress caused him to spark up another one.

"Nah, the streets been silent. I got a few niggas that want to see who did this dead," I replied as I nursed the whisky in my glass. It was hard to stay focused when I had personal shit happening to me too.

"Grizz, nigga, you been off your game. You would have been had a lead by now... What the fuck is up?" Uzi questioned me.

Manic turned and stared at me. He knew a little of what was going on, but not enough. "Man, I got a lot of personal shit going on. I'm trying to get my head in the game for Jah, but I got real shit happening in my home."

"Man, we all do. However, we got to put that shit to the back and find out who got at our nigga." J-Rell poured more drink into his glass. His ass was a little too upbeat for me.

"What the fuck do you have going on? You're never around and always ghost. He was found outside our trap. Where the fuck was you, and where's the money that he was supposed to pick up?"

J-Rell slugged his drink and set it down on the glass table in Uzi's office. "Man, I was running late and told one of those little niggas you all trust so much to hold it down. My girl been on my ass and shit, so I was arguing with her stupid ass and lost track of time. When I pulled up, I was gonna just go to the trap, grab the money, and put it in my car so I could go and see what happened. By the time I got there, the cops were already all up and through that shit."

"Cops never recovered any money," Uzi spoke.

"How you know?"

"Don't worry about it. I know they never recovered any money, and now I'm wondering where the fuck my money went."

"Hell if I know." Uzi knew cops, and he had cops on our team, so one of them put him on and told us that there was no money recovered.

"This shit is pissing me off. So basically, y'all sitting here and telling me that a damn ghost got at my brother?"

"Chill. I'll put my ear to the street and let you know what I find."

"Look, I'm 'bout to head out there now, and if I hear something I'll let you know." J-Rell got up and grabbed his wallet. He put it in his back pocket and then went over to dap Uzi. "Man, lil' bro gonna be straight. Have you heard anything?"

"Nah, his wife still playing games... My moms said she barked on her too."

"Damn, Tweeti not playing no games." He laughed. "On the real, hit me if you need anything... Holla at me."

"Bet," Uzi responded, and J-Rell left out of the office. We heard him making small talk with Remi before he headed out the door.

"Don't trust that nigga at all." Manic was the first to speak. I could tell something was off with him from the way he kept staring at him. It was as if he was trying to read him and figure out his thought process.

"You don't like no damn body." Uzi chuckled and took another pull from his blunt. "Your ass mean as hell."

"Nah, it's something about him and his story that's not making any sense to me. On the real, the shit don't make sense," Manic continued.

"If he hiding something, trust, it will come out. It always does. In the meantime, since you don't trust him, your job is to trail him."

"You sure you want him to follow him? This nigga might be moved to shoot him in the leg just because he didn't get ketchup on his burger. You know he's not wrapped too tight," I voiced. This nigga Manic was the last person that should be trailing somebody. He was the type to bring a dead body because he didn't like how they opened the door.

"Nah, I'll behave. I got two seeds coming, so I need to be alive and out of prison when they come." Uzi didn't know, but I knew all too much how he ended up in this situation. Manic told me everything and never held anything back.

He and Nisha should have been ended shit, but no, he wanted to keep fucking her, and now he had two chicks pregnant at the same time. I knew how much Nisha was in love with Manic. It was the main reason she continued to push him off and refused to be in a relationship with him. She thought by allowing him to get all his player ways out of him that he would be perfect for her, and that was far from the truth. Manic was once in love with her, and when she continued to turn him down, being in love turned to having love for her. Now they were expecting a baby while he was with Paisley and having a baby with her too.

"Man, I just be slanging this dick and making kids. I'm 'bout to be a father to two, and they not even from the same mama," he boasted like the shit was something to be proud about.

"And how's Paisley taking it?" Uzi just had to ask. I guess this little bit of drama was taking his mind off what was going on with Jah.

"She knows it was before me and her made it official, so she's taking it cool." He shrugged. "Right now, she's pissed at me because Nisha keeps calling and wanting me to do shit."

"Well, that's why niggas usually have one baby mama at a time, asshole," I butted in, and he flipped me the middle finger.

"Nah, on the real, Nisha do call a lot. And I be trying to be there for her because I know she lives alone and has her daughter, but damn, I'm tired of going to all these appointments. Half of them aren't doctor's appointments; she keeps making appointments for all these sonogram shits, and they expensive as hell. Three hundred dollars for a damn picture of a sick alien." He huffed and tossed his hamburger wrapper into the trash.

"Sundae is pregnant." Since he was talking about his babies coming, it seemed only right to talk about the one I had coming. "And Teyanna don't have fucking cancer."

"Told you. That bitch been a snake when you were in prison, and she's still a snake. How'd you find out?"

I explained to both of them how I found out, what happened with Sundae, and how I came to find out that I would be a father, and they stared at me blankly. The shit sounded like a Lifetime movie the more I sat and thought about it. Teyanna was really in there acting sick while I was doing my best to help save her life. While I was being everything for someone else, my girl needed me the most, and I turned my back on her. When Sundae told me shit, I didn't believe her and accused her of not taking her medicine. I knew that shit probably felt like a slap to the face.

"Well, damn. He certainly got me beat." Manic tossed his hands up and laughed. "Congrats, nigga. You may not be able to see your seed, but you still a father in my eyes."

"Fuck up."

"You killed that bitch, right?" Uzi stared at me.

"Nah, she still staying at my crib."

"Nigga, you stupid or dumb? Which one?" Manic hollered. I didn't know how to deal with the shit, so I kept Teyanna thinking shit was sweet between us.

When she called, I would tell her I was out handling business, and I'd be home soon. How the fuck was I supposed to bust her over the phone? If she suspected something, she would be ghost like she was all them other years ago. This time, I wanted this bitch to play for messing with my heart again. This bitch was the only person known to fuck me over and lived to talk about it. If that wasn't enough for her, she gonna come back into my life and do the shit again to me.

Who the fuck did some shit like that? What pissed me off the most wasn't about me; it was how she did Sundae. Sundae didn't deserve the shit Teyanna put her through. Walking around feeling crazy because someone you welcomed in your home decided to fuck with your life. Sundae had every right to be pissed with me with the way I played her.

"I'm going to deal with her. I just need to think how I'm going to approach her."

"Nigga, with a gun. You approach her with a fucking gun to her damn head. She came for your woman. You basically welcomed the enemy in your crib." Uzi leaned up and put his blunt out in the ashtray.

"I promise, let me handle this." I dialed Sundae's number and put the phone to my ear. The voicemail popped up, and I tossed my phone onto the table beside me. "Man, she won't even answer the phone for me."

"Nigga, she shouldn't. You got her all the way fucked up. Now I got two pregnant and hormonal chicks staying in my condo above my head."

"Nisha moved in with Paisley? How the fuck you swing that? That's why she's fucking pissed with you."

"Nah, Sundae moved in with Paisley. She moved in the other day and shit," he informed me, something his colorful ass should have been told me.

"Why the fuck wouldn't you tell me this when you found out?" I raised my voice, and he stared at me, unbothered.

"Wasn't my business, and I thought you knew, honestly." He shrugged.

"I need to head over there. I'll put my ear to the streets and let you know if I hear something." I dapped them both and headed out.

Now that I knew where she was staying, I could pop up and demand that she spoke to me. I knew I fucked up, and it was going to take some work to build our relationship and trust back, but I needed to know that I at least had a chance with the woman I loved. We were expecting a baby, and that was something bigger than the both of us. When I had kids, I imagined having my girl right there and being together. I came from a broken family, and I didn't want to give that to my seed. Me and Sundae needed to get it right and come together stronger than ever. Teyanna tried to break us apart, and it almost worked.

Manic and Uzi didn't understand why the hell Teyanna was still in my crib and I knew why. There was usually pleasure before the pain came. Right now, she was enjoying having the crib alone and waiting for me to come back to the crib. Little did she know was that the pain was going to come to her ass soon as I stepped over the threshold of the crib I shared with Sundae. When I thought about the stupid shit I did, I wanted to beat my own ass. Why the fuck did I fuck up what I had? We had finally got out of that awkward care giver and patient phase in our relationship. Sundae was happy and talking about us trying to start a family. I was seeing her smile and that spark that she missed. Shit was getting back together, and now shit was all off, and it was because I put my trust in the wrong person. I put my trust in the bitch that did me dirty years ago instead of the woman that had been there for me. Sundae had her shit with her, but you couldn't fake being real, and that was exactly what my baby was—real.

It didn't take me long to make it to Manic's building. I parked in the parking garage and walked a block to the building. The doorman knew who I was already and nodded while holding the door open for me. I pressed the floor and allowed the elevator to take me up to the desired floor. No lie, my heart was racing as I thought about coming face to face with Sundae. She just might punch the shit out of me or slam the door in my face. There was no telling what the fuck she would do to me. When I last saw her, she told me how hurt she was, and it wasn't the words that told me how hurt she was. It was her eyes that allowed me to look inside of her and see just how broken she was about the situation. I promised her that I would be there for her and never turn my back on her, and the first test that I got to prove the promise I made to her, I abandoned her and did the exact opposite.

My thoughts kept me so consumed that I looked up and was standing right in front the wooden oak door with the golden metal numbers *343*. I reached for the knocker and banged it against the door. It was silent for some time, and then I heard slippers sliding across the floor, heading toward the door. The peephole made noise, and then the door opened. Sundae was standing there dressed in a pair of jeans, a crop top, and her favorite fuzzy slippers. Her natural hair was out and pushed into a tight but bouncy ponytail. She appeared to look tired; still, she was the most beautiful person I'd seen in my entire life.

"What the fuck are you doing here, and why the fuck does Manic have a big mouth?" She rolled her neck and held the door open.

"Babe, let me talk to you."

"You've called, I'm sure. Did you get through to me?"

"Nah."

"Then that means that I don't want to talk to you. Why the hell are you here when you know that I don't want to talk or see you? What the fuck do you possibly have to say to me after all that has happened?"

"Can I come in?"

"Nope. Don't need your energy shifting the little bit of good energy that I do have left." She closed the door a little more.

Her body language and everything told me that she didn't want to be bothered with anything I said. Still, I couldn't leave without speaking to her. There was no telling the next time I would be able to lay eyes on her. Sundae would make it hell for me to get in contact with her, and she wouldn't hesitate to make sure that I never saw her again. I was a nigga that could find a penny I dropped when I was seven, but if Sundae decided to go ghost, she would make it where no one knew where she was. There were plenty of times I had to continue living life until she decided she wanted to see me. This time was different from all the other ones; she was carrying my seed this time.

"All I'm saying is I want to talk. You at least deserve to give me that."

"*Deserve?* I don't have to give you a damn thing except a bullet to the chest. You did this, not me, so I don't have to give you a damn thing. You got me all fucked up."

"We're having a baby. You don't think I deserve a sit down to talk about how things will go? Damn, all I'm asking is for a minute of your time."

She rolled her eyes, sucked her teeth, and swung her neck. "Meet me downstairs in the seating area."

"The fuck? What the hell is wrong with the couch behind you?"

"Like I said, I don't want anything that has to do with your energy. Meet me downstairs or hasta luego." She slammed the door, and I sighed.

Softly, I knocked on the door. "I'll meet you downstairs." I didn't hear anything on the other side of the door, so I headed downstairs.

Sundae's ass had me waiting for twenty minutes before she came downstairs. I looked her up and down to see if she switched clothes or something, because she took twenty damn minutes, and I wanted to see what the fuck took her so long? She plopped down in the arm chair across from me and crossed her legs while staring at me.

"What?" she asked.

"How are you?"

"I've been better." She shrugged.

"The baby?"

"How the hell am I supposed to know?"

"What the hell you mean, how the hell you're supposed to know? Shouldn't you be checking on it and shit? We can make an appointment and go."

She held her hand up. "I don't need you doing anything for me. I'm good with taking care of my damn self. How's your fake cancer patient?"

"I didn't come here to talk about her. I came to talk about us."

"Us?" She laughed hysterically. "There will never be another us again. Do you realize what you've done to me?" Her face turned serious.

"I know and I'm sorry."

"No, if you knew, then you wouldn't be sitting here talking about you're sorry. You would give me the space I need. You allowed another woman into our home under false pretenses. Not only did you do that, but you also allowed for her to fucking do shit to me and made excuses for her all while pointing the finger at me and accusing me of not taking my medicine. So, nah you don't know what you did to me."

Leaning up, I stared her in the face. "Baby, I understand, and I feel like a fool for the shit. All I was thinking about was helping her out. I swear if I would have known this shit was a lie, I wouldn't have allowed her to come into our home."

"You shouldn't have allowed the bitch to come in our home PERIODT!" she screamed. "That bitch wanted you from the moment she met me, even before. She saw what the hell we had and then saw the girl you loved and wanted to take her out the picture. Do you know I could have been committed for months again if my doctor didn't believe me? My fucking life could have been over because Lord knows I wouldn't have been able to survive six months in that place again. You allowed another woman to sit in my home and pick with me and fuck with my health. My health, Grizz. That's like allowing a nigga to move in with us and the nigga keep slicing you on the arm and you tell me, and I accuse you instead of dealing with the situation. That's exactly what you did to me and made no apologies for the shit."

When she broke everything down, I felt even more like shit. The shit she spoke was so true, and it was exactly what went on in our home, and I allowed the shit to happen. Sundae told me about shit, and I continued to accuse her of not taking her medicine. Like when Teyanna told me that Sundae sliced her, and I believed her and took that to Sundae's doctors. I didn't bother to ask her if she did it or not; I automatically accused her of stabbing Teyanna, and she hadn't laid a hand on that woman.

"Sundae, I'm prepared to spend the rest of our lives making it up to you. I fucked up, and I fucked up in a major way. You told me and even warned me, and I didn't listen to you. I should have, and we wouldn't be in this situation right now. She hurt you, and that's like her hurting me."

Her face screwed up, and she uncrossed her legs. "Yeah. Well, it's a little too late to feel like that. My mental health takes priority over everyone. For years, I've put others before my mental health, and I wasn't the best me that I could be. I'm no longer moving that way, and I can't stand to sit and look you in the face knowing that another bitch could come along and spit some lies in your ear, and you're accusing me of shit that I didn't do. I have a healing spirit, and I tend to attract those who are broken, but who the fuck is going to heal me? Not a damn soul."

It was clear that she wasn't going to take me back right away. I could tell the topic was pissing her off, and that was the last thing that I wanted to do to her. "Can we talk about the baby then? This baby is important to both of us, and I want to make sure you have a healthy pregnancy."

"Oh, no doubt I'll have a healthy pregnancy. I've gotten rid of those who are causing me stress. I won't keep you away from your child, and I won't deny you from coming to the appointments and stuff. However, when I choose to deal with you is when I choose to do so. Don't call, text, or just pop up here because you feel like it. I'm setting boundaries, and the first time you don't respect them, you're done."

"How am I supposed to know if you're good? What about money and shit?" She rolled her eyes.

"Deposit the money into my account. You don't need to see me to do that. In fact, maybe you should start looking for an apartment for me and the baby. I'm not moving back to Staten Island or back into that house, so you can let that dream go."

"I just bought that crib. You know how much money I would lose by putting it back on the market?"

She cleared her throat and looked straight at me. "No, you didn't hear me. I said I wouldn't be living in that house. I never said you couldn't. Do as you please; I don't care. All I know is that Paisley has a baby she needs to prepare for, and I don't want to halt her process by staying in the room that's supposed to be her nursery. Find us an apartment, pay for it, and give me *all* of the damn keys."

This woman could have told me to take a gun and shoot myself in the foot and that was what the hell I would have been doing. Sundae was making it very clear that she wanted no relationship or anything to do with me, and she made the shit *crystal* clear. It was hard hearing her talk about wanting her own apartment. The house we shared in Staten Island was ours, and now she wanted nothing to do with it. I mean, I understood why she didn't want anything to do with it. Teyanna tainted that shit with all that she had done. Long as she was allowing me to be there during her pregnancy, I was going to take what I could get.

"I'll work on getting that done, baby. You know I love you, right?"

"Thanks," was all she said, and she headed back to the elevator. This shit was crazy, and I hated where we were. I needed to deal with the situation with Teyanna, and I needed to do the shit soon. I had to get my woman back, and I needed to get her back quickly. Being without her was too long.

6

MANIC

"Everything looks good here. I'm happy the cramping has stopped, and you're staying off your feet as much as you can. We're not out the woods yet. We have a long road ahead, and we may hit some bumps, but long as the end result is a healthy baby, then we're on the right track," the doctor informed us as he moved the sonogram machine around Paisley's stomach.

"You can tell if she'll have the baby early or not?" I asked him. Usually, I was the one to make Paisley smile or laugh when she was nervous. However, whenever we stepped into this office, the roles switched. She was the one there for me because I was nervous. No visit was a good visit because I constantly worried about my baby. Would Paisley make it to her due date? Would she have more complications than she already had? Shit, a bunch of shit kept me worried when she got on that examination table.

"We won't know that just yet. All we can do is to continue monitoring her progress with each visit. Now, as you both know, the sex rule is still in effect. I know this is hard, but we don't want anything to happen to baby. Any kind of arousal can stimulate contractions."

"We're good. I'm not thinking about it, and my child's health is more important than having sex." Paisley was the first to speak.

"Great. Now, for the fun part of the visit. Do you want to see what you're having?" He smiled at both of us.

"Hell yeah!" I damn near shouted. Nisha was having some little party to find out the gender of our baby, but at least I could find out the gender of one now.

"What about you, Paisley?"

"I guess so." She smiled nervously.

He moved the machine around a bit and then hit a few buttons before he turned to look at the both of us. We were holding hands and staring at each other. Paisley went to look away, and I used my other hand to turn her face back toward me.

"Nah, I want to look you in the face while we find out the sex of our child." She smiled at me and continued to stare into my eyes. We've calmed down on the bickering about Nisha. I put Nisha's number on silent so that it didn't ring when she called. When I saw I had a missed call from her, I would text her to be sure she was straight. Paisley meant a lot to me, and she was who I had been wanting for a long time, so I needed to fix what was wrong with us. Nisha was my baby mama, but Paisley was my woman, and we had a baby coming that needed the both of us.

"It's a little girl," the doctor said, and I had the biggest smile on my face. A tear fell down Paisley's face as she looked up at me and held my hand tighter.

"What the hell am I going to do with a little girl? God, you up there playing jokes, huh?" I laughed and bent down and kissed her on the lips and held the side of her face. My baby was bringing my baby girl into the world.

"Are you happy? Did you want a boy?"

"Baby, I don't care what you have... Long as this baby is healthy, I don't care." I continued to kiss her on the lips. "Are you happy?"

"Yes, I'm happy that I'm going to have a daughter. I get a second chance to right all the wrongs my mother did with me." She sniffled and wiped her eyes.

"Yeah, that tends to be the best part of parenthood." The doctor smiled. "I'll have this printed out and sent to the mobile number in your file. Pick up the medicine at the front and continue to take it easy. I'll see you in two weeks. Any complications, you go straight to the ER and give me a call, okay?"

"Will do. Thanks, Doctor." She shook his hand and he left the room. I helped her down from the table, and she pulled her jeans up some and her shirt down. "A daughter. Wow."

"This shit makes my heart happy and complete. I'm thinking Maniacita." I tossed out a baby name that might fit our baby.

"What the hell? Mitchell, you need to go and sit the hell down somewhere. We're naming her Aubree." She smiled. "I've wanted to name Sayana that, but her mama picked that weird ass name."

"You was picking baby names with the bitch that fucked your man?" Each time she told me more and more about her past relationship with Rome, I couldn't believe she put up with half the shit she did.

"Yeah. She came over, and we did that and planned the baby shower. I hated every minute of it, but I pretended to love it so I didn't get slapped into the coffee table in front of Syria."

I put my arm around her shoulder and walked out of the exam room. We picked up her prescription and headed out the building. "Baby, do you think I treat you bad?"

"What? No, why would you think that?"

"'Cause I don't want you to feel like you need to put up with shit I do because you live in my condo and I pay for shit. You have an option, and you don't have to put up with no shit when it comes from a man... you hear?"

"I hear you." She smiled.

"Good," I told her before opening the door. She slid inside of it and smiled when she saw the gift box on the seat.

She waited for me to get into the car before she spoke with a huge smile on her face. "What is this?" She smiled widely.

"You didn't think I forgot your birthday? I know the appointment was dumb early and you were cranky and shit, but I didn't forget."

"Baby, I swear I was going to cry myself to sleep tonight. My mama sent me a dry text and no one else called me. Sundae jumped in my bed this morning and said it, but no one else."

"I would never forget the day that God blessed this world with my soulmate. Open the box," I told her and pulled away from the curb. I was taking her out to eat and pampering her all day. I'd been knee deep in the streets, and we hadn't spent much time together, and it was my fault. As always, she didn't complain, bicker, or blow my phone up. She stayed up waiting for me to come in the crib to call to make sure I was home safe. For that, she deserved for the day to be all about her.

"Finding out about Aubree was the biggest and best gift I could have gotten." She smiled as she untied the ribbon. She opened the box and smiled again. "It's beautiful, but what does this mean?"

"It means I want to marry you one day. Not today, tomorrow, or next week, but one day. One day when we've gotten to know each other more, grown with our daughter, and really get the hang of this relationship shit, we'll take that walk down the aisle together."

"I really can't stand you." Her voice was shaky as she stared down at the beautiful princess cut ring with a pink diamond. "Did you know about the baby before me?"

"Nah, I got this because you love pink. This couldn't have been perfect timing." I smirked, and she reached over and kissed me on the cheek.

"I really appreciate you, Mitchell. I love you so much." She smiled at me, and I continued to drive.

"You know I'm not done, right?"

"Lordy, what else do you have up your sleeve?" She giggled and slid the ring onto her finger.

"We're going to Atlantic City right now where I got us a suite to chill out. We don't have to gamble or nothing; we can sit in our suite and enjoy each other without interruptions." I smiled at her.

Paisley didn't hound me about the time I spent in the streets, and it was what I appreciated about her the most. Still, that didn't mean I was going to sit back and ignore her and the fact that I neglected her at times to run the streets. My baby's cries were silent, but I heard them loud and clear, so I was giving her all of me.

"Baby, this is amazing. I'm excited to just lay next to you, eat, and see what AC is really about. I've never been." She rubbed my shoulders.

"I got one more thing."

"Mitchell! Enough."

"I've been riding around in your present this entire time. This Bentley truck is yours. I got it for you before your birthday and planned to surprise you."

Her hands flew to her mouth, and she turned in her seat and stared at me with wide glossy eyes. "Are you kidding me right now? A Bentley truck, Mitchell... Why?"

"Because you're my dream girl, and she deserves a dream car. Paisley, I told you all I want to do is make you happy. I don't care about nothing else except making you happy as fuck. You cried for so long that now all I want to see is a smile on your face." I touched her face. "Stop being such a cry baby."

"I can't help it." She sniffled, and I laughed. "I'm really trying, but my face is leaking." She continued to sniffle.

We drove to Atlantic City talking about everything under the sun. We spoke about the future we wanted for our baby girl and how we wanted to raise her up. Paisley wanted her to do dance, cheer, and all that girly shit. I didn't care about none of that shit, but I bet my ass be front row with a fucking cheer skirt on if that meant supporting my baby girl. I didn't have family besides Grizz, so to have a small family meant a lot to me. I wasn't going to front and say that it wasn't different because it was. I had two people in my life that depended on me to bring home the bacon and make sure our family wasn't broken. I also had two people depending on me to do the right thing. If I fucked up and cheated, just like I spent time building my small family, I would break my family too.

"So, what do you think about Sundae staying with me? We haven't spoke about it after she moved in, and I wanted to get your thoughts. I know I didn't ask, but I just wanted her out of her mother's house." She brought up the subject of Sundae.

"No way. Sundae's family, so I don't care. You don't have to ask me a damn thing either. That's your crib, and you can have whoever you want over."

"She said that Grizz is getting her an apartment soon, so she won't be there long," she informed me. Grizz would give that girl a million dollars if she asked.

"Word? He trying to get back in good with her."

"Well, he needs to be buying her much more than a

condo. What he put that woman through should be considered murder or something." She rolled her eyes.

"Yeah, but everyone deserves a second chance, feel me?"

"Second chances or not, he still needs to work for it. That woman was literally losing her damn mind, and no one could tell her why. Then the one person she should have been able to count on let her down big time."

"Alright, we not even going to get deep into this shit," I called the topic up. Grizz fucked up, and I was about to pay for his mistakes.

"Sorry. I just feel her pain."

"I could tell. You over here rolling your neck and getting loud like I did some shit to you or something." I chuckled.

"Promise me one thing."

"What's that?"

"Don't hurt me... ever."

I took her hand in mine and looked at her briefly before I spoke. "I promise you that I won't."

"Thank you." She kissed my hand and put her head back on the headrest. I knew in five minutes, she was about to be knocked out. Our appointment was early as fuck this morning, and if I could, I would take a nap too.

"Baby, wake up." I gently shook her. The valet driver already had the keys, and Paisley was still in here snoring like she was in her bed.

"Give me ten more minutes," she groaned, and I scooped her out the car. Her eyes widened, and she looked me in mine. "What are you doing?"

"We're here, and you over there snoozing and shit."

"Well, I'm tired as hell. What we gonna eat?" She started talking about food like she always did when she woke up from a nap. The fridge in her apartment looked like she fed a family of six when it was only just her.

"We can get checked in and then try this new restaurant downstairs."

"Can I get a steak?"

I nodded and checked into the hotel with her still in my arms. "Yeah, baby. You gotta feed my baby girl."

"I know. All she wanna do is eat and have me sleeping. I need to find me a job or something."

"Nah, you gonna sit and let my baby bake. We don't need you stressing or no shit like that." I shot down her dreams real quick. Once she got a job, then the stress came, and I didn't feel like dealing with that shit. Especially not when my child's life was at risk.

"Fine." She agreed and dropped the subject.

This wasn't the first time that Paisley had mentioned something about going back to work. For some reason, she felt like she had to be doing something other than chilling. I wasn't worried about her just chilling and making sure we had a healthy baby. Paisley seemed to be the only one tripping about not working or pulling her weight around the crib. I grabbed the keys with my free hand and continued to carry Paisley up to our suite. I spared no expense to make sure my baby had the best for her birthday. We couldn't fuck, but we could enjoy each other's company and grub on all this damn food I was sure she was about to order.

"You really went all out for me. I appreciate everything you've done and are going to do for me. Sometimes I wish there was a way I could repay you back for everything you've done for me, Mitchell." She kissed me on the cheek and laid her head on my shoulder.

"Real men do shit because of their hearts, not because what they're going to get in return. Everything I've done or plan to do for you is because I love you and want you to be happy. You don't need to repay for me anything that I do because I'm doing it because I love you," I told her, and she kissed me on the lips.

"I appreciate you so much, babe," she told me as we exited off the elevator and made our way down to the double doors at the end of the hallway.

She pushed the card into the slot, and the doors allowed us access into the suite. Upon opening the door, you could see the waterfront of Atlantic City. There were lights from the different hotel buildings. The room had floor to ceiling windows with white leather furniture facing toward the view. To the right, there was a chef's kitchen with state-of-the-art cooking shit in there. To the left, there was a long twelve-person dining table made up with two place mats already waiting on us. On both sides, there were master suites with a balcony, bathroom, and huge bedrooms.

"Good afternoon. I'm your chef. I have lunch on the stove, and it will be done in a few moments. You can take a seat at the kitchen table, and I'll bring you both a strawberry pecan salad with a mango vinaigrette." The short white man came from behind the massive island in the kitchen.

"How are you doing? I'm Paisley, and that salad sounds delicious." Paisley nudged me to place her down and then shook the man's hand. "Sit over there?" She pointed to the table, and the chef shook his head.

We washed our hands and made our way over to the dining room table. I pulled out the seat and admired Paisley's fat ass as she plopped it down in the cushioned seat. Damn, the pregnancy had her gaining weight everywhere except in her stomach. When she had no clothes on you could see a small belly, but the shit looked like she was bloated instead of actually being pregnant. I low-key wanted to ask her where the fuck was my baby because I wanted to see a big swollen stomach and rub all over it.

"This is really nice, baby. It's so beautiful here," she

complimented as she looked around the room. I would do anything for her, so this was nothing. If I could give Paisley the world, I would. It was because she never expected shit from me. She didn't stress me for materialistic shit; all she wanted was my time. How could I be mad at that?

"Anything for you, babe." I winked and rolled out the cloth onto my lap. This chef was real fancy. He must didn't know a nigga like me. I was the type to go ahead and eat with my hands and smack my lips at the same time.

"What are we going to do? You know the doctor told me to take it easy."

"And that's what we're going to do. We don't need to leave this suite. I have a prenatal massage lined up for you tomorrow morning. You need to just chill out and shit."

"Well, I'll get to relax with you right by my side. I'm excited to spend time with just us," she stressed. I knew with me being gone all the time that it stressed her out. Especially when I brushed off her feelings whenever she brought it up to me. A nigga needed to do better, or I was going to lose the person that I cared for the most.

MY PHONE CONTINUED TO BUZZ ON THE NIGHT TABLE beside the bed. After eating all that food yesterday, me and Paisley explored each other's body like no other. When you couldn't fuck, you got real creative on how to bust a nut. Even with me not sticking my dick in her, my dick had busted three nuts back to back. I was realizing that I didn't have to choke her ass out for me to bust a nut. Paisley was showing me how to be soft when touching her and showing me her favorite places. This morning, we woke up, ate breakfast, and she sucked my dick on the balcony while I read the morning paper. Afterward, we brought it to the bedroom, and I sucked on her clit and nipples until she creamed in my mouth four times. The doctor advised against anything that could cause her to climax, but shit, we were sexually frustrated.

We spent most of the day sleeping, eating, and watching TV, cuddling together. A few hours ago, we had fell asleep watching some weird ass Netflix show that Paisley wanted to watch. I silenced my phone and rolled back over with my eyes closed. Sleep was what I needed right now, and whoever that was blowing my phone up was going to have to understand that.

"Mitchell, your work phone is blowing up. Turn it off," Paisley complained and slapped me before pulling the covers back up over her head.

I rolled over and grabbed the burner phone that sat next to my iPhone and flipped it open. Placing it to my ear, I scratched my balls and yawned. "Who this?"

"What you mean who this? I've been calling you, and you can't answer your damn phone?" Nisha's voice blared through the other line.

"The fuck you mean? I've been sleep, Nisha. I'm fucking tired too. I don't have the right to sleep?" I barked back and leaned up in the bed.

Here I was all mellow and calm, and this bitch had to call going off on me. The fuck she meant? I had to get some fucking sleep too. "I mean, I've been calling you since two this afternoon, and you haven't picked up your phone once."

"Dead all that shit." I cut her short. "Something wrong with you or the baby?" If she was calling me like this, then it had better be a fucking emergency or something.

"I want some chicken and rice from the Spanish spot. I can't leave because I twisted my ankle earlier taking my daughter to daycare," she whined in the phone, which wasn't like Nisha at all.

"Have somebody go get the shit for you. I'll send you the bread if you need it."

"I don't have nobody to bring it to me, and I kind of need you to go pick up my daughter too," she decided to toss in there like it wasn't nothing.

"Call her daddy. And while he's dropping her off, you need to tell him to bring you some food too. Damn, you needed me to figure that out for you."

"All of that would have been simple if her daddy was out of prison. He got knocked, and he's looking at some serious numbers. What am I supposed to do without his child support? You know that's how I was living."

All I knew was that Nisha fucked around and got money. How she got her money wasn't my care or concern. She wasn't in my pockets asking for money, so I didn't give a fuck where she got it from. I commended her for holding down her shit and never begging a nigga for money. Hearing her on the phone whine about how the fuck she was going to live without her baby father's money had me looking at her slightly different.

"Get a job, start a business... shit, I don't know. Do something that doesn't take me away from getting sleep that I need."

"I'm hungry with a twisted ankle, and you can't even help me? Bet if I was Paisley, you would have been running your ass over here to help," she snapped through the phone in a jealous rage.

"You serious right now?" I leaned up in the bed. She had me so fucked up with the shit she wanted to wake me up with. I treated both of them fair, and I couldn't stand that she always tossed that in my fucking face.

"Yes." She sniffled. "I'm alone, and I can tell this baby is going to come second to everything you have over there with Paisley." She cried through the phone.

Snatching the blankets off my body, I stood up, and

Paisley rose up while wiping her eyes. "Babe, you okay?" She looked around the room.

"Go back to bed, baby. I'll be back," I told her while I held the phone to my ear and handled the situation with Nisha. "You want me to pick up Khamazia, go get you food, and bring her to you with the food? Where the fuck she at, Nisha?"

"In Harlem at my cousin's house. She was watching her for me last night," she replied quickly.

"Bet. Text me the address." I ended the call and placed my phone down on the dresser while I went to grab some sweats and a shirt.

"Where are you going?" I heard Paisley's voice behind me. The last thing I wanted to get into was a fight with my girl over trying to help my baby mama. You hear how fucked up that shit sounded. I was happy that God saw me fit to be the father of two babies at once, but damn, couldn't he had blessed Paisley with twins or something? Why they had to be from two baby mothers?

"I gotta go pick up Nisha's daughter and bring her Spanish food because her ankle is sprained or some shit like that." I ran down what I had just found out during me and Nisha's annoying ass conversation.

"What the hell? So she doesn't have any family? Doesn't she know that we're on vacation for my birthday?" Paisley raised her voice and got up off the bed.

I slipped my feet into my Gucci slides and turned toward my pregnant girlfriend who had this scowl on her face. If looks could kill, I would have been a pool of blood on these stained oak floors.

"It's complicated, Nis... Paisley," I slipped up, and I knew I fucked up when I almost called her Nisha.

"And now you're calling me by this bitch's name!" she screamed.

I walked over to her and tried to calm her down, and she snatched her hands away from me. "I'm sorry, babe. I got a lot of shit on my mind, and I fucked up. Nisha don't have family, and she needs me to help her out. I mean, I'm her baby father, so I gotta help her out."

"I'm always going to come second to this hoe, right?" She stood with her arms folded in nothing but her bra and panties. Her little bloated stomach was on full display.

"When I turn my head to the left slightly, your stomach really growing," I randomly replied.

"What? Manic, stop fucking trying to switch the fucking subject. I'm always going to come second to her in this relationship, right?"

"You know that's not true."

"Well, it's my birthday weekend, and you're rushing off to bring this bitch her daughter and her food!"

"And you want me to ignore her? She talking about she sprained her ankle or some shit. Nisha don't have family like that, and the little bit of family she do have ain't worth shit, so I gotta be there for her too. You're important to me, Pais, so please stop making me choose."

"Whatever." She grabbed her robe off the chair and put it on and aggressively tied the robe around her waist. "You grabbing *my* car keys to go and run and play errand boy for this bitch. Go ahead and do you, but don't bring your ass back to this hotel."

"How the fuck you gonna tell me that I can't come back here?"

"You heard what the hell I said," she repeated and slammed the bathroom door. I sighed and headed toward the door. Something had to fucking give because I couldn't keep doing this shit. The only time I had peace was when I was fucking alone. Between Nisha and Paisley, I was going to lay up in a bed beside Jah's ass.

7

J-RELL

Everybody was running around trying to figure out who the fuck tried to end Jah, and I was laughing. These niggas were nowhere near close to who the fuck shot him. I had to admit, with the McKnight name, I didn't think I would be able to pull this shit off or get away with it. Here it was two weeks later, and this nigga Jah was still on ventilators and shit. Uzi was so busy trying to find out who had something to do with this that he wasn't focused on the streets. Money had slowed up, and everybody wanted to know when the fuck our next shipment would come in. It seemed like it wasn't a priority when it came to Uzi, and his people were pissed with him. Shit, if I hadn't taken all that money the night I shot Jah, I would have been fucking complaining too. Time meant money, and all these niggas had was time, but no money was coming in.

Me and Dallas had been arguing like crazy, so I sent her ass to Miami for the week. She was getting on my nerves about staying home all day and me being gone all day. It was a little over a hundred thousand dollars in that money I took, and that wasn't enough for me to start my own shit. I mean, I

78

could buy some product, but it wouldn't be enough to start an empire and wipe out the McKnight name. It was still too hot, so right now, I was chilling and spending money slowly so they wouldn't be suspicious.

"Why are you here?" Ashley's voice brought me from my thoughts. I sat on the front of my whip in front of her parents' realtor office.

She had on a black pencil skirt that framed her thick ass thighs. The way she shifted her weight on her heels with her arms folded, I licked my lips, wanting to feel in-between her thighs again. Man, she had really grown up since I was gone, and she was far from that young girl I fell in love with years ago.

"I mean, you haven't seen me in years, and this how you show love? Damn." I laughed and looked down at her.

"And it wasn't like you came and found me when you got out. I heard you got a girlfriend, and I got a man, so there is no need for this little reunion."

"I wouldn't have had to go get me a new girl if you didn't fuck Jah McKnight while I was locked up."

Her face dropped as she stared at me. "Why are you bringing that up again?" She leaned closer and whispered in a harsh tone like there was somebody else out on this sidewalk with us.

"You hurt me, and then you got the nerve to act like I fucked you over." I continued. I usually sped past here and kept it pushing. Today, I decided to stop and let her know how the fuck I felt.

With Dallas off my nerves, I had time to handle some business that I had been putting off for the past year. Ashley was running around here living life like she didn't fuck me over. She was lucky she wasn't meeting the same fate that Jah was. I came to remind her ass about the foul shit she was doing when I was locked up. While she was running around living life with her new man, I needed her to know that the foul shit she did was still on my mind, and like today, if I felt like coming by her job to reminisce, I could.

"You really need to go. That was while we weren't together, and you need to learn to leave the past alone." She tried to walk away, and I pulled her back.

"Nah, you owe me this."

She snatched her hand back and stared at me with hate in her eyes. When did she start hating me? How the fuck was she mad at me when she was the one who did me wrong? "I don't owe you a damn thing." She straightened her clothes.

"Why did you leave me in there to rot?"

"You didn't tell me you were going to commit a crime and get put away for years. We're even."

I had to laugh to keep from slapping this bitch in the mouth like a child. She was acting more childish than ever, and I was trying really hard to control myself. "And that was my fault. I shouldn't have left you out here all alone."

"You hurt me too, J-Rell. I wanted you to be here for me, and you weren't. What the hell was I supposed to do? Jah was there for me when you weren't, and it wasn't right, but I needed him."

"So you fuck another nigga and think I'm supposed to be good with that? I don't give a fuck that you needed me. Bitch, you fucked and had a baby with another nigga on me."

"Jah wasn't the father of my baby."

"You lying like hell."

"I'm serious." She sniffled. Now she wanted to throw on these baby ass tears because she had to confess the foul shit she had done in the past. "There was another man during that time and he's the father of my baby. You nor Jah are the father, and it's none of your business what I did with my child."

"Fuck outta here... That's the nigga's baby, and you're lying."

"Do you think that Jah would have his seed out in this world and wouldn't know about it? The dude I had the baby by was a one-night stand. We never spoke or saw each other after that night. My son is happy, healthy, and well taken care of with his new family. My parents don't even know about him. You're coming around here stirring up the past, for what?"

"Ashley, you have a call on line three." The receptionist stuck her head out of the front door.

She turned around briefly to address the receptionist. "Tell them to hold; I'm coming." She sighed and then turned back to me. "What we had was beautiful. I was young and dumb then, and I regret doing you the way I did, but that was the past. I hear you're happy and moved on, and that's all I'm trying to do right now. Take care of yourself." She reached in and kissed me on the cheek before she headed back into the office.

After all these years, I wanted to know why and what I had did for her to do me the way she did. I finally got the closure I sat in my cell praying for, and now I realized that I was trying to wife a hoe. Ashley's ass was a fucking hoe and was fucking every damn body when I was locked up. They say it's those good girls that were the freak hoes, and I now realized that was exactly what Ashley's ass was.

"Ash?" I called out behind her, and she turned around and looked at me.

"You broke my heart, bitch!" I yelled and walked around and got into my car. As I pulled off, her mouth was wide as hell in shock. Deep down, I still loved the hell out of that girl and could never lay a hand on her.

Soon as I turned the corner, Dakota's damn name popped across my screen. I wished I sent her dumb ass away with her sister, but they weren't talking right now. I hit the button on my steering wheel and cringed as I heard her ass whining about something.

"All I do is sit in this damn apartment and take care of this damn baby," she whined on the phone, and I sighed because it was the same complaint she always gave. That's what the fuck mothers did, and all she did was complain about it.

"You're a mother."

"And you're a fucking father. I don't never see you around here doing a damn thing for this baby. My sister is in Miami, living her best life, and I'm here with this crying baby all damn day." She began crying.

All the hell she did was cry about every damn thing. I was so tired of hearing her complain about being a mother to our son. She was so happy when she was pregnant because she thought she had the upper hand on her sister. Turns out, Dallas wasn't interested in being a mother right now. All she wanted to do was pop fucking pills and party in Miami. These bitches both were going to drive me damn crazy.

"I'll come chill with you and the baby later. Right now, I'm running around and handling shit. You know how it is since Jah got hit."

"How is he? Did he die yet?"

"Damn, you cold. Nah, he still holding on. I'll check you later, and make sure you cook something."

"Ugh, I wanna feel your cock right inside of me," she moaned on the phone. "Please hurry." She cooed, and I ended the call.

Bitch was crying about being a mother a few minutes ago, but now she was happy about getting some dick. I shook my head and continued to head out to do these rounds. There wasn't much for me to do; all I was doing was being nosy and seeing which trap I could try and take over. It wasn't about the house, but more about his workers. Those niggas were hungry, and they wanted to make money, so that's what would motivate them to switch teams. Uzi had his brother, then his fiancée had lost their baby, so shit was falling down the tubes for his ass. While he was dealing with his shit, I needed to build my empire.

THE DAMN CONDO WAS A FUCKING MESS WHEN DAKOTA LET me in. It smelled like cigarette smoke and baby shit. Clothes, shoes, and baby shit was all over the condo. Dishes were piled up in the kitchen sink, and this bitch had the nerve to have the baby laid in a dirty ass bassinet. The sheet she had in it had milk stains from previous feedings. I could smell that he needed a diaper change, and I hadn't even been in this bitch for a cool two minutes.

"The house is a mess. Jah stopped having the housekeeper come over, and now it's a mess." She sighed.

"You never picked up a broom or a mop? I know for sure I've seen your sister do it a few times." Dakota and Dallas were sisters but opposites. They did everything differently, and it was the reason I chose to marry one and just fuck the other one. Dakota wasn't wife or mother material. She needed to be back in a trailer home doing meth or something, because the way this crib smelled, it made no sense. If Jah saw his shit looking like this, he probably would have died just from the smell.

"I've been busy being a mother to our child. You forget that?"

"Nah, the way you got my son in this dirty ass crib, I can't tell." I picked my sleeping son up and went to her room. That shit was worse than the front of the damn house. Dirty diapers were balled up on the nightstand and she had shit every damn where. "Where's his damn clothes at and shit?"

"In the dresser over there." She laid out on the bed like she was about to get some dick. Hell, if I knew this was how she lived, I wouldn't have been holding a baby right now because I wouldn't have fucked her ass.

I went and grabbed some clean clothes, baby wash, and all the shit he needed before going into the dirty ass bathroom. There was hair every damn where like she was a fucking dog or

something. Hair in the sink, behind the toilet, and in the drain of the tub. Luckily, there was a baby tub inside the regular tub already. I held my son with one hand and cleaned out his little tub the best I could before sitting his fat self in there.

My son was so damn cute and chubby. Dakota wasn't shit as a mother, but this little baby hadn't missed a meal yet. I washed him up quickly and then wrapped him up in the duck towel. When I got back into the room, Dakota was snoring. I quickly put my son into his clothes and then fed him. As bad as a woman she was, I knew motherhood had her tired because no woman should sound the way she did. Not once did she wake up when I covered her body and dragged the bassinet into the bedroom. By the time I finished feeding him, he was back asleep in his clean bassinet, and Dakota was still sprawled out on her mountain of clothes on the bed. I kissed my son and headed out. I didn't plan on being here long, but spending that small amount of time with my son felt like everything. I made a mental note to take Dakota for custody soon as I was up on my feet from building this empire.

🎋 8 🎋

TWEETI

"I 'm glad that you are finally out of that damn hospital room. You need some damn fresh air and some good food." Evelyn smacked on her turkey burger.

Three weeks and nothing had changed with Jahquel. The only thing that had changed was the shifts that nurses changed. I was so tired of fucking being in that hospital room that I was angry. I resented Jah being involved in the streets and us ever fighting over that lying ass bitch. Everything that had went on in the past few months, I resented. All I could think of was my baby boy, husband, and myself being locked away in our home. Physically, I was sitting here on a patio at some fancy restaurant in Manhattan, but mentally, I was at the hospital with my husband. Emory had been pushing for the family to be up there to pray, so I gave them their moment alone. The entire McKnight family had me pretty disgusted right now, right along with my sister.

"Well, I'm not really feeling festive right now." I sighed and leaned back in my chair. The salad I had couldn't have had more Caesar on it, and it was missing parmesan. My

85

appetite wasn't there, and I didn't want to leave the hospital, but Evelyn forced me.

"You really need to speak to your sister. Did she tell you what happened?" My mother raised her eyebrow and stared at me. "You haven't spoke to her?"

"What happened?" Since the day I kicked both her and Uzi out Jah's hospital room, I hadn't seen Remi or spoke to her at all. I was so tired of her and the selfish shit she pulled.

Since we were children, it had always been about Remi. She was the skinny sister, and everyone always gravitated toward her more than me. I loved my sister, but she was selfish as hell. That was the reason that she and Uzi had lasted as long as they did. He was able to put up with the tantrums she threw because he dealt with the shit from his own mother. I wasn't Parrish McKnight, and I didn't have to put up with that shit. She was selfish to announce her pregnancy while my husband laid in the bed a few feet away, fighting for his life. She acted as if nothing was wrong with what she had done either. Then to act like her baby not having a father was more important than mine pissed me clean off. It didn't matter if Uzi went on a rampage around the city over Jah or he fucking decided to walk to the store, he was a target because of his name and his street ranking. Remi made everything about herself, and right now, I didn't need that shit in my life right now.

"She lost the baby," my mother revealed to me. I was sad that she experienced a miscarriage. The baby I had lost still was fresh on my mind too.

"I'm sorry she had to go through that. Tell her I love her, and she's strong and can try again."

"Do you hear yourself? You sound like an automatic machine greeting, Tweeti. Your sister needs you, and you want me to tell her that you love her."

"Ma, I have a lot going on too. Why do I need to drop

everything because Remi had a miscarriage? She damn sure didn't stop her trip when I had mine. Life moves on; she'll get pregnant again. I'm not sure I'll get that same chance because my husband is lying in a hospital bed with no improvement in three weeks!" I yelled.

A few patrons turned to look our way and then went back to their meal. My mother wanted me to drop everything I had to run and be by Remi's side. It sucked that she had to go through this, but it was life. While she was dealing with that, it wasn't like I was sitting here playing with my hands. I hadn't seen my son in the past week, Jah was still in the hospital, and I felt fucking alone. She had a whole team of support over there, and my mother was on my case because I decided to choose me and my family first.

"She has Wynner and Emory over there every day, but they're not her family," she protested, and I didn't want to hear anything else she had to say.

"Soon as she marries Uzi, she'll become their family. I'm glad they're there for her but couldn't come and be by my side. Despite how mean and shit I was to Jah while we were going through our issues, he stuck by my side the entire time."

Me and Wynner used to be close once upon a time ago. It wasn't until I started telling her to choose herself first and stop waiting around for her damn husband to make moves for them. Once I started telling her that she was putting her all into her marriage and motherhood and nothing into herself, that's when I became the bad guy. The same with Emory. When I started speaking back and not listening to her opinions, that's when I wasn't invited to the monthly spa outing. Remi was the prized possession because she didn't argue, have an opinion, or analyze their life like they did others. Wynner and Emory could look at your life, insert themselves in your shit, and then had the nerve to be mad when you did the same shit to them.

"That's not the point. You and your sister need to be there for each other. If you don't want to go over to her house, that's fine. Just give your sister a call and let her know you're thinking about her."

"I'll think about it." I sighed and stabbed my fork into the lettuce. This food wasn't what I fucking wanted. Hell, I didn't want anything that was happening to my life right now. Then I had to find out that my sister miscarried her first baby.

"Have you given any thought about moving Jahquel to the hospital in Staten Island? It's been three weeks, Tweeti, and you haven't been home once."

"I really don't know. The doctor told me that he thinks it would be good since we live there, and the travel wouldn't be so much."

"Taz needs you. I'm not complaining about caring for my grandbaby because I love him so much, but I know he also needs you."

"Yeah, I know. He cried last week when I had to leave you guys at the park."

"See. I feel like the bad guy keeping you away from him or something." She chuckled. My mother had come back and really stepped into being there for me. I found myself feeling like I should pinch myself because of how helpful she was being.

"I know. How are you doing?"

"I'm fine. Sundae comes over on Tuesdays to watch him while I attend my meetings. You don't need to worry about me. I'm more worried about you and all that you have going on." She touched my hand.

"I know how you handle stress and don't want you to feel like I'm putting too much on your plate."

"I'm learning how to handle my stress. Taz isn't stress; he

makes me feel happy. It makes me think of your sister." She smiled.

"She's so happy and loves to be the center of attention like her big head older sister," I joked to lighten the mood.

Wynner told me that if my mother ever got her life together, she didn't want Prize to meet her. At the time, I was so angry with my mother that I agreed with her. Why should she see her baby? She abandoned her while she was in the NICU being weaned off the drugs she put in her body while pregnant. Now seeing my mother and how much pain was in her face when we spoke about Prize, I knew that idea wasn't a good one. She at least deserved some closure when it came to her own child. She knew she would never get her back, but being able to see the baby she birthed would give her the well-needed closure she needed to continue with her sobriety.

"I can imagine. You know, you complain about your sister, and you're the same. When you want to be, you're self-centered." She laughed, and I rolled my eyes at her.

There was some truth to it, but I was self-centered when it came to my marriage. Jah spoiled me rotten, and I may have taken advantage of that. However, I was never selfish when it came to the people I loved and cared about. Remi should have been there for me as my big sister, not Uzi's fiancée. I needed her more than he did, and she didn't understand that. In that moment, she was supposed to put her personal shit aside and be there for me, and she failed.

"I bet." I sighed and continued to poke at my salad. Me and my mother sat and chatted for a few more before Sundae sent me a message and told me she was picking me up.

As nice as it was to catch up with my mother, I was ready to get back up to the hospital to see if anything else changed with Jah. My mother paid the bill, and I kissed her on the cheek as I left the restaurant. The talk and time away were much needed away from the hospital. Jah's family had their time, and now it was time for them to leave so I could put lotion on his feet like I did every night. A few times, his toes moved, and the doctors told me that was probably just his nerves. I was tired of waiting for him to wake up. Jahquel McKnight knew how impatient I was, so if he knew what was good for him, his ass better had wake up now, because I couldn't take too much of this shit.

"That sun looks good on your skin... I can't remember the last time I saw you outside of that hospital room." Sundae cracked a joke. With all that she had going on, she still managed to be there for me when I needed her.

"Girl, shut up. What you been doing?" I asked as I buckled my seat belt and waved goodbye to my mother. She had my car, so I wasn't worried about how she was going to get home.

"Trying to move on. I'm just trying to put one foot right in front of the other and get back on track. I have this baby depending on me." She smiled and pulled away from the curb.

Sundae needed to remain in a good place for herself and this baby. She didn't need the stress and headache that Grizz was going to provide. The only goals she had was to have a healthy baby and deliver that baby with a healthy and happy mental space. Grizz had a lot to deal with before he could even try and make his relationship with Sundae work again. If he really wanted the best for her, he would leave her alone and give her time to sort out how she was going to do with her life.

"I'm glad that you're in a good place."

"God blessed me to carry a baby, and I don't want to fuck it up. Now that my doctor has me on a new dose of medicine, I feel better."

"And living with Paisley?"

"It's cool. If she didn't have to prepare for her baby, I wouldn't mind living with her for a bit longer."

"All that baby need is a damn bassinet. You don't need a whole room, and I know that. Taz had this whole nursery, and he didn't sleep in it until he was around nine months. Even then, I don't think he slept the whole night in there."

Nurseries were just for pregnant women to have something to do. In my opinion, that room was a waste of money and time. I sat in there a few times and breastfed Taz, but other than that, I was in my bed with my breast propped right in his mouth. Paisley wouldn't need the whole room, and she needed a roommate more than she knew. She was battling with being alone and then trying to find her place in Manic's life. With what she told me, she could use someone there with her.

"I need to sit down and have a talk with her. She's with Manic, and I don't want her to feel like I'm trying to cramp her style."

"And from what I heard, he lives upstairs, so all she has to do is go upstairs. Paisley needs to establish some independence without Manic anyway."

"You always trying to tell somebody what to do with their life." Sundae laughed.

She was laughing, but I was serious. Paisley moved from one person to the next. The difference between Rome and Manic was that Manic was paying for everything in Paisley's life. At least with her ex, she was working a job. With Manic, she had to depend on solely him because she was having a complicated pregnancy and couldn't work. I just wanted her to depend on herself and not a man. I was going to be good with or without Jah. Yes, it would hurt if he died, but I would live and be able to provide for both me and my son. Paisley was so used to depending on a man that she wouldn't know what the hell to do with herself.

"I'm serious though. You can teach her a lot, Dae. You were good with Grizz, and you're going to be good after. I'm not worried about you at all. Now, Grizz... his ass probably walking around like a big ass dummy."

"He's a real dummy. The only time we talk is when he sends a message and asks how I'm doing. I reply and tell him and then that's it. I told him he better not pull up to the house without speaking to me first."

"I'm so happy that you're moving in the right direction and not letting this get you down." I touched her hand.

"I have no choice. I'm not going to lie; if I wasn't pregnant, I would have fallen into a deep depression." Her voice started to get shaky. "I love him, Tweet. I thought we were going to spend our lives together." She sniffled and quickly wiped her eyes.

"I'm sorry, babe. I know it's hard, and you're trying to keep it all together." I comforted her as I dug into my purse and grabbed my ringing cell phone.

When I saw Emory's name pop across my screen, all I could do was roll my damn eyes. I didn't want to speak to her ass at all. My purpose of leaving before they all got up there was to avoid seeing any of them. Still, she was up there with Jah, and more than likely she was calling to update me on something the nurse or doctor must have told her.

"Yeah?" I answered the phone dryly. The whole McKnight family was on my shit list. I was so pissed with all of them, including my sister.

"He's awake! Jahquel is awake!" she screamed through the phone, and my heart sped up. "Tweeti? You there?"

"I'm here," I spoke calmly, yet my body was in complete shock, and I wanted to scream out. What kept me from screaming was Sundae driving. I didn't want her to crash because the way I was going to scream was sure to scare the shit out of her.

"I'm on my way now," I replied and ended the call quickly. My hands were shaking as I set my phone on my lap.

Sundae looked over at me and then back at the street. "Well, are you going to tell me what that was about or continue to stare into space?"

"Jah woke up," I revealed.

Sundae hit the brakes, and my head jerked forward. "What the fuck?"

"Girl, you should have hollered that shit so I could have hit the gas on this bitch!" she squealed in happiness.

"He's awake, but what if he's not the same?" I worried. He was shot in his head, and the doctors made sure to remind me that he could have brain damage. My fear was Jahquel waking up and couldn't talk or wouldn't know who me or his family was.

"Jahquel McKnight is going to be the same. You married that stubborn asshole; you know his ass is the same."

I sighed and leaned back in the chair. I was so nervous about what the hell was going on and what I was going to walk into.

Sundae broke all the laws getting us to the hospital. As much as I wanted to see Jah awake, I was so scared too. I was scared that I was going to walk into the room to a shell of my husband. Fear must have been written all over my face because Sundae put her hands in mine as we made our way upstairs. She occasionally gave me a squeeze and smiled at me as the elevator got to the designated floor. Soon as we stepped off the elevator, I noticed Shad in the hallway on the phone. From his body language and his hush tone, you could tell he was talking to another woman. When he saw me and Sundae step off the elevator, he rushed off the phone and headed over to the both of us.

"How you feeling?" he asked and leaned in to kiss me on the cheek. "You can tell you've lost some weight. Have you been eating?" I lied. Shad was the only McKnight that I could tolerate. He never had much to say, and he didn't pry in our business unlike Emory's ass. She was always in everybody's business except her own.

"I'm good. Is he really awake?" I looked up at him, and he nodded his head and pushed me forward.

"I'll be in there in a bit. I need to wrap up this phone call." He hugged me as me and Sundae continued down the hallway.

My damn hands were sweaty, my heart was beating, and I felt like any minute, my damn heart was going to jump out my chest to run down the hall. When we got near his room, the doctors were in the room along with all the family. All eyes were on me as I walked in the room. That's when I saw him. Jah's eyes were wide open. I rushed over to his side and touched his hand. He looked at me weird and started making noises as if he didn't know who I was and had brain damage.

"Oh my God. Is he going to be like this forever?" I gasped as he rolled his eyes to the back of his head and started moving his head from side to side. He still had the tube down his throat, so he couldn't speak, but you could hear him making sounds.

"Jahquel McKnight, stop playing with your wife like that," Emory scolded with a smile on her face, and Jah smiled as best he could. "He's fine, Tweeti. He knows who you are, and from what the doctor says, he doesn't see any signs of brain damage."

"I swear I can't stand you, Jahquel!" I hollered and bent down and kissed him on the cheek. "Baby, I missed you so much. I thought you were gone." Tears welled in my eyes.

He wanted to talk, and I could tell, because he kept trying to touch the tube. "Jahquel, we'll leave that in for a few more days, and if everything is good, we'll remove it," the doctor said from the corner.

He stared me in the eyes, pleading with me. "Is it possible for him to get it taken out now?"

"No. He has been up for a little over an hour, and complications can occur, and we would hate to have to intubated him again. If he does well these next few days, we'll take him off and treat him for the sore throat I'm sure he'll have," he told me. "We'll have someone come in to get some blood from him. On a serious note, I'm not a praying man, but God was looking out for your husband. It's a miracle that he's awake but he's also aware, and before we test him, he seems like he's all there."

"I want to thank you for being in my corner and listening to all my crazy theories on how to treat him. You didn't shut me out like most doctors; you listened to me. I appreciate that more than you know." I gently touched his shoulder.

"I'm doing my job. You're a good wife. I've seen your face more than I've seen my wife. You never left his side, and I made sure to tell him that. The one second you leave, he opens his eyes." He chuckled. "You have a good woman here." He pointed to me, and Jah smirked.

I smiled and went back over and rubbed his hands. Everything we had been going through went out the window. God set me straight and showed me who and what was important to me. Jah and my son were what was important to me, and I needed to make sure they both knew it. He tried to tell me everything was a lie, and I didn't believe him. My chest started to hurt when I thought about almost losing him.

"Man, I can't wait until you take that shit out your throat. You all looking pitiful," Uzi joked and held his brother's hand.

I looked around, and Remi wasn't up there with him. Part of me wondered where she was. Jah slapped my hand, and I turned my attention to him. My sister was a second thought when it came to my husband. He was alive, and this was a second chance for us both to get it together. Remi had her fiancé she had to worry about, and I had my husband that I needed to worry about.

Jah still had the tube in his mouth, and he was supposed to get it out tomorrow. I was so excited that he was doing better. Because of the tube, they kept him reclined back, and I knew he wanted to be propped up. Like always, I continued to rub his skin down with oil so it didn't become dry. Everyone came up to the hospital to see him and catch up. Uzi came up every day and sat and spoke to his brother. Jah couldn't speak back, but you could tell he understood everything that his brother was talking about. Taz wanted to see his dad so bad, but the hospital didn't allow kids up here under twelve. I knew there were some ways I could have got around that; still, I didn't want to run the risk that my son would get sick or something.

Jah was taking his mid-noon nap while I sat on the couch and flipped through a magazine. I wanted to call my sister and talk to her. Things in my life wasn't as hectic, so I could take time to sit and talk to her about what happened between us. It had been a month since everything happened, and we still hadn't said anything to each other. She went through a miscarriage, and I wasn't there for her. If we weren't arguing, I would have been the first person at the hospital by her side. My mother didn't want to admit that I was being selfish and thinking of myself. Here I was using Jah as an excuse for the way I was treating my sister. Yes, she was selfish and thought the world revolved around her, but she was still my big sister. Jah's phone started ringing, and I grabbed it before it woke him up. It had been dead since everything went down, but he had motioned for Uzi to put it on the charger yesterday.

Zuri came across the screen, so I stepped out the room and answered the phone. I looked back before I closed the door behind me and placed the phone to my ear.

"Hello?"

"Hey, is this Jah's wife?"

"Uh huh."

"I heard what happened, and I've been trying to get in contact with somebody. His brother hasn't returned my calls, and I just want to make sure that he's alright... Is he okay?" She sounded genuinely concerned because she was speaking so damn fast I couldn't make out half of what the hell she was saying.

"He woke up two days ago, and they want to make sure he's fine before removing the tube from his throat. I'm sorry. His phone has been dead, and it was the last thing that was on my mind."

"No, that's understandable. I've been going crazy because I didn't know if he was alive or dead, and his daughters keep asking for him."

It was another stab in the stomach that I didn't give Jah his first daughter. This would be something that would always bother me. I was his wife, and I wanted to be the only person giving him babies. As much as it bothered me, I had to check myself and realize that this child was made and born before me and him got together. This wasn't the child's fault, and from what Jah told me, he lied about the damn DNA test. Jah had a huge heart, so it didn't shock me that he decided to take responsibility for both girls, even though he only fathered one.

"The girls can't visit because they're too young, but you can come up. I can text you the information," I offered.

"I would like that. The girls really wanted to bring him up a picture they made him," she told me. It was like the more she mentioned the girls, the more I realized that Jahquel had other children than just Taz.

"Can I ask you a question?"

"Sure. One second," she told me and removed her face from the phone. I could hear her telling the girls to go play outside in muffled tones. "I'm back. The girls were getting too loud."

"Has Jah ever introduced my son to your daughters?"

"No. He was supposed to and then he never did. I guess he was waiting to speak to you about it."

"Oh, okay. Thank you."

"I do want them to meet. They're siblings, and I want them to have a close bond. Even if they're from different mothers. I was an only child, and I'm glad my girls have each other, but knowing that Jahquel has a son, that means my daughters have a baby brother. They know all about him and want to meet him so bad."

"I'm being honest with you. I don't think I'm ready to take that step yet."

"Tweeti, it's your call. Whenever you're ready, we're here. I don't want to push my kids on you if you're not ready." I appreciated that she was understanding and understood that I wasn't ready yet. Shit was happening too fast, and that was something I was going to have deal with; still, it didn't mean that I had to deal with it right now.

"Thank you. Make sure to bring the girl's picture. I'm sure he would love to see it," I reminded her.

"Of course. I'll see you soon," she told me, and we ended the call.

I stood out the room for a bit before I opened the door and closed it behind me. Jah was up and staring at the ceiling. When he heard the door, he looked toward me and waved his hand. I held his phone up. Soon as he saw the phone, his eyes got wide, and he looked shocked.

"Calm down. Zuri called to check on you. She said the girls made you a picture, and she's going to bring it up here when she comes up." He nodded his head and pointed to the tube. "One more day. Get some more rest before she comes," I demanded and pulled the covers over his feet.

He closed his eyes, and I sat in the chair beside him, thinking about the life that I was going to have to live. My husband had twin daughters and a son. There would be weekends that they had to come over to our house, and I had to have a relationship with them. I couldn't be one of those women who hated the child because of the situation. They had nothing to do with the situation; they were babies. The more I thought about it, the more I realized that I had to get my mind together to deal with our new life. God spared my husband's life, so the least I could do is try to make this blended family thing work. If I found out that he and Zuri slept together during our break, then I was going to beat both their asses, and that was on baby.

❦ 9 ❦

PAISLEY

Thank God for Sundae. She was able to come and pick me up soon as Manic had left. I couldn't believe he chose to run after Nisha instead of being there for me. What did this woman have over him? He was willing to drive back to New York from New Jersey to fucking take her food and get her daughter? Two days had gone by since this entire thing went down, and I was still pissed with him. I should have meant more than Nisha on the phone whining about him not doing for her. I understood he was in the middle of things and felt like he had to do for us both, but what made me different from her was that I was his actual girlfriend. That should have counted for something, and it didn't. He treated me like I was just his baby mama too, and that shit hurt more than he knew. Something inside of me told me that we were rushing things, and I continued to go with the flow. I shouldn't have been in a relationship with Manic this soon. We should have waited and continued to get to know each other.

Now, I was sitting in the middle of my bed with ice cream and watching Hallmark movies, feeling like shit. Manic had been calling me every day and every damn hour, and I refused to answer the phone. When he knocked on the door, I told Sundae to tell him I wasn't here, or if she was gone, I wouldn't answer. For once, I wanted to be put first, and it felt like that was never going to happen. Nisha was going to make sure that she inserted herself into our lives. Now that I knew she was in love with him, that meant that she was trying to push me out the picture. She didn't give a fuck about me or my baby and wanted us gone. Nisha wanted Manic to herself and that proved that when he walked out our hotel suite to take her food and pick her daughter up.

"Let's go out shopping or something." Sundae came into my room and plopped on the bed. Sundae was the perfect roommate. She cooked, cleaned, and was quiet. I barely heard a peep out of her unless she dropped a bowl while cooking. I actually didn't mind her living here full-time, even when her baby came.

"I'm not in the mood. If you do go, bring me some food back."

"As if you haven't been eating enough. You really need to get out the house and have some fun. All you do is sit in here and cry over these damn sappy movies," she pointed out.

I hid the box of tissues under the blanket. "First of all, you don't know my life." I laughed. She was right. All I did was sit in this house, crying over these corny movies, and walking to the kitchen to refill my cup or bowl once it was empty.

"I do, and that's why I'm begging you to get out the damn house. I'm already depressed because of my current situation, but I'm really depressed sitting in here with your sniffling every damn second."

"Girl, these damn movies have me bawling my eyes out." I laughed and sniffled because I had just finished crying. "This one movie was abou—"

"Yeah, I don't give a damn about none of that. I think we should go baby shopping or something. I'm early, but still." She sighed.

"I don't want to shop until I deliver this baby."

Sundae nodded her head, understanding, and climbed up further on the bed. "I know. You're nervous, but that baby will enter the world. I promise you that." She hugged me tightly. "Now, go on and get in the shower so we can go out."

"Where are we going? I don't feel like leaving the house." I whined as I laid back on the bed.

"Girl, we're going to get our nails done with Remi. My nails need to be filled in, and I want to get some leggings and stuff." Sundae looked at her nails and then at me with a sad face.

"Fine." I sighed.

I'd been in the house, and I did need to pamper myself a little. Doing a little retail therapy and pampering was probably just what I needed at the moment. Leaving the house and doing anything seemed nearly impossible. I was always tired, hungry, and sometimes, I just didn't want to leave my little bubble. Was that so wrong of me to do?

"Thank you! I'm going to change, and I'll be back in here, and you better not still be in this bed," she stood up and warned me before she left out of my room.

I sat there for a few minutes before I got up and pulled myself together. The baby weight was coming on because I could feel it when I pulled on jeans or wore a shirt that was once loose. This pregnancy thing seemed like it was happening fast, and I didn't know what the hell to do. Someone's mother? I was going to be responsible for another human being. That was what was so crazy to me. I was going to have a baby in a few short months with Manic, and we had a slew of problems to solve. After pulling on some jeans, a white tee, and Adidas sneakers, I tossed some water in my hair and watched it curl up before sliding a hat on top.

Sundae was dressed and sitting in the kitchen when I came out my bedroom. She was dressed in a crop top, leggings, and a pair of flip flops. Her natural hair was pulled into a ponytail. I sighed in relief that we weren't doing anything crazy because this was the best she was going to get from me today. The only reason I wanted to go was because I was going to try and convince her to stop and get me Chinese food before we came back into the house.

"Well damn, you are really dressed down."

"Says the girl with leggings and a crop top." I rolled my eyes and went into the fridge. "Which salon are we going to?"

"The one Remi and Tweeti go to. They're still not talking, and I want to cheer Remi up. You know she just miscarried, right?"

"I didn't. Wow, and she was excited."

"Uh huh. She just needs something to take her mind off things, so I figured we can go get our nails done and then go shopping after."

"Sounds like a plan. Do I bring it up or...?" I allowed my voice to trail off. If I lost my baby, I wouldn't want any more talking about it, so I wanted to know how I should approach the situation.

"If she brings it up, then talk about it. I wasn't going to bring it up because we're both pregnant, and it must be hard on her."

"Yeah, I understand. Is Tweeti coming along?" We were so happy when we found out that Jah had woken up and was doing good. For someone who was shot in the head and was able to be up and know who everyone was, that was nothing except God.

"She and Remi are going through a rough time. Plus, I know she's going to be spending every waking moment with

Jah. They're moving him to the ICU since he's about to get the tube removed. They kept it in a few extra days."

"I need to go up there and see the both of them."

"Yeah, well if you stop crying up in your room over those movies, you would have time," she joked.

"I'm going to make a girl's night, and we're gonna watch two of them. I bet you start crying too," I challenged.

"Deal. But, umm... I want to talk to you about something." Her facial expression became serious.

Leaning on the counter, I looked into her eyes, and she looked right into my eyes. "I know this situation was supposed to be temporary, but I didn't think that I would love living with you this quick. I would love to live here a little longer, and I can pay you or Manic rent."

She took the words out of my mouth. I'd been trying to think of ways to bring it up to her, but I figured she had her mind set on getting her own place. My baby wasn't due for quite some time, and even then, the baby wouldn't be sleeping in that spare room. Sundae was the perfect roommate, and I actually liked having someone here other than myself.

"No, I actually wanted to talk to you about it. I've been looking for ways to afford this place."

"Eh, don't you live here rent free?"

"Yes, but I'm tired of men doing for me. I want to take care of myself and pull my own weight. Mitchell doesn't mind, and he says it all the time, but I feel like a child."

"You have a high-risk pregnancy. How are you going to work?"

"I found some virtual assistant work online the other day. The pay is decent, and it'll allow me to work from bed and still be able to pay some bills too."

All I did was sit in the bed on my laptop and watch TV. Manic pissed me off so bad that when I came home, I started looking for work. I didn't care what the job was; I just wanted to stop depending on him. While searching job boards, I found a virtual assistant position for a publishing company. The pay was better than my previous job, so I knew I would be able to help with rent, food, and other stuff I needed.

"He's not going to be happy about this." She folded her arms and smirked. "You told me that he shuts you down anytime you mention something about going back to work."

"Yeah, but I *need* this, Sundae. I have to do this or else our entire relationship will be built on him taking care of me. I'm tired of having to ask him for money to do something or waiting around and waiting on him to do something. Hell, when I do shop for my baby, I want to go and buy them something with the money out of my account."

"No, I get it. I'm just not there yet. Grizz gonna pay out the ass, and I'll be damned if I get a job, but we're different." She laughed.

"I feel like I sound like I'm being selfish or a brat."

"No, you want to be independent, and there's nothing wrong with that. You went from being in one relationship where you worked, but still depended on a man, and then another where the man treats you like a queen, but you still want to find your own independence. There's nothing wrong with that," Sundae replied. The way she put it made me feel ten times better about the email I was about to send to the owner of the publishing company. She was waiting on my response, and I told her I needed to think about it.

"Thanks, Sundae."

"Of course. Now, I was thinking this apartment needs a woman's touch. You know, since I'm going to be living here and stuff."

"I kind of left it the same because I didn't want to touch his stuff."

"Well, next month we'll be tenants. We can do whatever

we want." She smirked and grabbed her purse. "Let's go!" she called behind me. I quickly typed the end of the message and pressed the send button before grabbing my purse and heading out the apartment behind her.

We ended up at this expensive nail bar that served champagne and fruits. I was used to getting my nails done in a crowded Chinese salon. You know, the ones where they're busy and the owner still keeps taking damn people. It was one of the main reasons I hated to even go to the nail salon. I always felt like there was so much more that I could be doing instead of sitting in a nail chair getting my nail color changed.

"How you been feeling?" Sundae broke the silence as we put our feet into the marble foot tub. I pressed the button and started the massage and listened to Remi.

"I'm actually good. You know, after losing the baby, I realized that I don't want to have any kids," she revealed, and me and Sundae both looked shocked as hell.

"Rem, you can't let one incident scare you into not having kids." Sundae touched her leg. "It will happen again for the both of you."

"This is the second time me and Parrish have been pregnant. I aborted the first baby because it happened during the time I had got shot, and we were dealing with that," she explained, and my eyes widened at the fact that she threw out that she was shot nonchalantly. "This time was unexpected, and I was going to have it because Parrish has been in my ear about having another one now that Paris is gearing up to start applying for colleges and stuff."

"What makes you not want to have any kids?"

"I don't think I'm a kid person. I love my nephew and stuff, but I don't see myself being a mother, and I'm fine with that." She guzzled down the rest of her champagne then popped a grape into her mouth. "I just wish everyone else understood that."

"He wants more kids though. Do you think he'll still marry you?"

She shrugged her shoulders. "If he doesn't, then it wasn't meant to be. I'm not going to have a baby because that's what *supposed* to happen next. I'll have a baby when I'm ready to. And if I ever have the urge to have a baby of my own, that's fine too."

She was right. People assumed that women were made to just get married, serve men, and pop babies out. Sometimes, women didn't have the maternal bone in their bodies, and that was fine. Often times, they were fine with just being an aunt or godmother. Instead of people respecting that, they continued to push babies into their face. Just because Remi was about to be married didn't mean she was obligated to have a baby next. Now, I didn't know how that situation was going to work with her future husband wanting more kids and she didn't. That situation sounded like something I didn't want to be involved in at all.

"You definitely need to go and talk to Uzi about it. Rem, he wants more kids, and you don't, so you need to at least tell him before getting married." Sundae took the words out my mouth.

"Oh, I will. We're supposed to meet up this week for drinks and dinner. Now that Jah is doing better, he's not as stressed. He's still out there looking for this damn person, but he agreed to dinner, so I'm down."

"Hope it works out for you, Remi."

"Thank you, love. I'm just trying to push through. Have any of you spoke to my big-headed little sister?"

Sundae raised her hand. "I spoke to her yesterday. Why? You both gonna stop being stubborn and talk?"

"I'll talk to her when she's done being a bitch to me." Remi rolled her eyes and got her glass filled with more champagne.

"She's under a lot of stress too," I added.

"We'll talk eventually. Tweeti is stubborn, and I just needed time away to deal with her." She rolled her eyes. "Love my sister to death though."

"You both have been doing this for years. When are the both of you going to grow up and realize everything isn't about the two of you?" Remi didn't seem offended by Sundae's words. I guess it was because they had been friends for so long that she could pretty much say anything and the other understood where it was coming from.

My phone rang, and I tuned out their conversation and answered the phone. "Yes, I'm fine. Yep, your baby is cool, and we're both fine." I answered all the questions I knew Mitchell was about to ask me. This was the first time I had answered the phone since I left the hotel. The only reason I answered was because I felt it was selfish to keep ignoring his calls and not at least update him on how I was doing.

"Why the fuck you doing all this shit?" he barked through the phone. "All I'm trying to do is love the shit out of you and maybe stick the tip in!" he continued to holler in my ear. His ass was so loud that both Remi and Sundae stopped their conversation and looked my way.

"You good?" Sundae checked.

I pressed the mute button because he was still going on and on. "I'm fine. He's wondering why I've been ignoring him."

"Oh, okay. Handle that then." She laughed.

I took the phone off mute and placed the phone back to my ear. "First of all, you need to lower your voice. I'm not Nisha or any other rag headed bitch you're used to dealing with. Second, we both need to sit down and talk, so I'll come to your apartment when I get home."

"Where you at?"

"In my skin." I ended the call.

My feelings for Manic were very deep. I loved this man, and it was crazy because it hadn't been that long. Even with all of the feelings I had for him, I knew that we needed to take a break. Things got too serious very quick, and I just needed a breather. I didn't want the pressure of being his girlfriend and all that extra stuff. All I wanted to be was his baby mama right now. All the extra stuff needed to go away until I was ready to deal with all of it. He wasn't going to take the news well, and I knew he would cut up. Let's be real; it wasn't Manic unless he was cutting up. Still, he had to understand my position and my feelings. When he chose to run behind Nisha and disregard my birthday weekend, that told me everything I needed to know right then and there. If it was too hard for him to choose me over his baby mama, then I was going to make the decision for him. Now, both me and Nisha were on level playing field.

Hanging out with the girls was cool, but all I thought about was some vegetable lo mien and my bed. Then, the harping thought of sitting down and talking to Manic was shadowing over me. After we got through with our nails, we went shopping, and now I was sitting in the back of an Uber heading home. Sundae and Remi were going to grab a bite to eat, and I wasn't in the mood. Not to mention, I was cramping, so I knew I better head home. Whenever I was on my feet for too long, the cramping started, and that was my reminder that nothing was more important than my child. Besides putting myself first, I also had to learn how to put my child first as well. Sundae offered to drive me home, and I told her I was fine, and I would catch an Uber. We were a block away from the building, and the Chinese food I made the driver stop for was smelling all too good.

I thanked the driver and headed into the building. Pressing Manic's floor, I shifted my weight from foot to foot. I had to pee like a damn Kentucky race horse, and this slow ass elevator was taking forever to make it to his floor. When it finally got to the floor, I sped down the hall and banged on his door. He opened with his drawers on and looked at me confused.

"You ignore me and then got the nerve to bang on my d—"

"Move! I have to pee." I shoved the shit out of him and rushed to the bathroom. I was so in a rush that I set the food on the floor beside me as I took a piss.

"Where you been?" He opened the bathroom door and stood there with his arms crossed. Privacy was another language to him. Shoving the door closed with my left foot, I leaned forward and locked it. "You acting like I haven't seen your shit before."

Flushing the toilet, I washed my hands and grabbed my food before I opened the door back up and rolled my eyes at him. "We need to talk," I told him and went to sit on the couch.

"About Nisha? I fucked up, and I'm sorry that I did that. Even when I left, I felt like shit for doing that. I had plans to make it up to you, but you were gone when I got back."

"That's the issue right there. You wouldn't have to make up anything if you didn't do shit in the first place. That call from Nisha should have been ended when she asked you to pick up her child. That child isn't yours, and her problems aren't yours unless it has something to do with the child in her stomach."

"You right," he agreed and sat on the couch across from the one I was sitting on. "You're absolutely right. Me and Nisha go back, so I feel like she's family, and I can't let her down."

"Family don't fuck each other. You killed that family excuse when the both of you decided to fuck. You're saying

I'm right, but soon as she calls, you'll go running to do whatever she needs."

"All I'm trying to do is make the both of you happy. I want
this shit to work more than anything, but you both have to
give me a break."

Oh, he wanted someone to give him a break? "Speaking of
a break... I think we need to take one."

His jaw dropped when the words came out of my mouth.
"Nah, don't do this shit. You not about to play with my heart
and shit, Paisley."

"I don't want to play with either of our hearts. Things
moved too quick, and I think we just need to step back and
catch a breath."

He rose to his feet and stared at me. "The fuck you think
this is? A fucking marathon? You can't pick and choose when
the fuck you want to be with me."

"Yes the fuck I can. Especially when my supposed nigga
keeps choosing a bitch he used to fuck over me. As far as the
apartment, I found a little job to work from home, so I can
start paying rent. Sundae is staying, and she'll have her half of
the rent too. We'd like the utilities in our name too."

He started doing his usual pacing and ran his hand
through his hair. "Man, I feel like you just fucking ripped my
heart out, fucked it, and tossed it out the window while
driving eighty miles per hours on I-95 with a trunk full
of coke."

"Really? You're being dramatic right now, but you'll see
that it's for the best. If the man I'm with can't put me first,
then I need to be smart enough to put myself first. You
taught me that, remember?"

"Not to use against me, the fuck? And I put you first. It's
one time you're bringing up, Paisley. Damn!"

"No, each time Nisha calls, you're running. I'm tired of

feeling second when it comes to me and you. I still love you, and you know that."

"Yeah." He plopped down on the couch as I stood up and grabbed my food.

"You'll be very involved in the baby's life. I promise." I smiled and headed out the door. He took it better than I thought he would. Right now, it was time for me to get my life together and stop being worried about a relationship. The situation with him and Nisha would bother me as long as we were in a relationship together. I needed to remove myself from that situation quick, fast, and in a hurry. What we both needed to focus on was this baby that was in my stomach--nothing else.

MY PHONE BLARED LOUDLY ON THE NIGHT TABLE BESIDE me. I turned my light on and grabbed the loud ass phone and put the phone to my ear. I squinted and looked at the clock before sliding my finger across the screen. The number wasn't Manic's number, so I sighed in relief and held the phone to my ear. It was three in the morning, and this unknown number was calling my damn phone.

"Hello?" I answered irritated. After spending the day getting pampered and shopping, I was tired. My body felt like I had run a damn marathon or something.

"Paisley... I need you get to my house now." I heard Ms. Vee's voice on the other end of the phone.

I sat up in the bed and jumped when I felt someone in the bed with me. It was Manic laying in the bed with me. "Ms. Vee, hold on," I told her and muted the phone. I slapped the dog shit out of Manic, and he jumped up and grabbed the loaded gun on the night table beside him before he opened his eyes.

"Yo, who want it?" He held the gun up in the air, and I ducked down.

"Put the damn gun down! Why are you here!" I screamed, and Sundae came rushing into my room.

"Oh, it's him." She waved and left back out the room.

"Paisley... Paisley..." I heard on the muted line.

"I'll deal with you in a minute." I mushed him in the head and unmuted the phone and placed it to my ear. "Sorry, Ms. Vee. What's going on?"

I met Syria's mother a few times. More times than I actually cared to meet her. A few times, she was the one dropping Sayana off to me because Syria had said she was coming back and never did. She was a sweet woman, into the church, and stayed to herself. I always questioned how she had a damn hoe like Syria for a daughter.

"Can you come to my mother's house?" she questioned.

"Why? It's three in the morning. What is going on?" I was becoming worried because she was talking in circles.

"Syria and Rome were killed in an accident tonight," she revealed, and for the first time, I could hear the tears in her voice. "My baby is gone, Paisley." She sobbed into the phone.

Rome was dead. My heart dropped, and I felt like I couldn't breathe for a second. I squeezed the phone and tried to catch my breath, but it seemed like it wasn't working. A while back, I had an anxiety attack at work, and Dallas talked me through calming myself down. All I heard was her voice, and I calmed myself down quickly.

"What do you mean an accident?"

"They both were drinking, and Rome was driving. The car was crushed and... my baby is just gone." She started to cry again.

"I'm so sorry, Ms. Vee." There was nothing else for me to say. Rome was gone. He was dead, and I felt so sad. Like, my heart felt like it was ripped out of my chest and tossed on the floor. I shouldn't have given a fuck about the man that physically, mentally, and emotionally abused me for years, but I couldn't help it. I felt fucking sad and started to cry on the phone with Ms. Vee.

"Can you get to my mother's house?"

"Yes. I'll be there. Give me some time to pull myself together."

"Understandable," she told me, and we ended the call.

Manic was sitting beside me confused. I didn't bother to address him. Whipping the covers off my legs, I went to the closet and pulled something quick to throw on. I was so sad that I felt like I wanted to die too. It was a strange feeling that I felt, and I didn't think anyone, except someone who had been in my situation, could understand. Not all of our times were bad. We had good times too. Like the time when we went food shopping and forgot the mustard. It was the main purpose for the random shopping trip, and we forgot it. We sat in the kitchen on the floor laughing for hours and passing each other a blunt. Thinking back, it was probably because we were so high when we went shopping that, that's why we forgot the mustard.

"You gonna fill me in on what happened?"

"Why are you in my house?"

He saw my face and crawled to the bottom of the bed with quickness. "Why you crying? What happened?" He touched my hand and pulled me close.

"Rome is dead." I sobbed and broke down.

I just knew he was going to curse, get mad, and make me feel like shit for crying over this man, but his actions surprised me. He pulled me down into his arms and cradled me like a baby as he consoled me. I was mad that he had got into my damn bed a minute ago, but right now, I was happy that he was here for me.

"I'm sorry, baby," he kept repeating over and over again as

I sobbed into his chest. I wasn't only crying for myself, but for his family too. He had a daughter, and she would never see her father ever again. My heart hurt so bad that I just wanted to place it on the night table so I didn't feel like the pain I felt.

Manic drove me to Queens where Syria's grandmother lived. Soon as I stepped out the car, the rain fell down on me. I looked up at the sky and wiped away a tear that slid down my cheek. Manic held the umbrella over us as we stood on the stoop and waited for someone to answer the door. Ms. Vee answered the door, and from the look on her face, she had been crying nonstop like I had been. She pulled me into a big bear hug and kissed me on the cheek.

"I'm so sorry, baby. You're strong, and you're going to get through this," she told me and patted me on the back once more before we broke our embrace.

"I'm sorry, Ms. Vee. Syria loved you more than anything." I didn't know that, but it seemed like it would be the best thing to say back.

"Thank you, hunny bun." She offered a weak smile. "Come on and let me get a pot of coffee on," she said and made her way into the kitchen.

"Sit down. Let me go help her," I told Manic, and he nodded while taking a seat.

Ms. Vee made her way around the kitchen while sniffling. "What can I do to help?"

"Oh, baby, you don't need to do a thing. I'll whip this up and be out in a second," she tried to convince herself more than me.

"Ms. Vee, I know you know that me and Rome had broken up, right?"

She sat on the wooden stool and nodded her head. "Syria had told me. She and Rome were working on getting back together for the baby. They were buying this big house up in

Delaware. She was finally getting it together for the baby." She sniffled and wiped her nose with a balled-up tissue.

"I'm glad that he was turning his life around." I pulled up the other stool and sat in front of her. "I guess I'm confused as to why I'm here?"

"You're Sayana's legal guardian, Paisley," she revealed, and I cocked my head to the side, confused by what the hell she was saying.

"Yeah, but that was so she could get insurance from my job. I don't work there anymore. I'm sure Syria and Rome got her new insurance by now."

"It's either she goes into foster care or with you. I'm five years from seventy and can't raise no baby. I just moved back with my mother because her health is declining. I love my granddaughter, but I can't physically or financially do it," she told me and stared into my eyes.

"How am I going to raise her alone? I'm pregnant with my own, and I'm going through a complicated pregnancy myself."

"Paisley, you damn near raised that little girl alone without the help of Rome nor Syria. While they ran around town partying, you were home raising that child. Congratulations on the new baby, but I know you'll do right by her." She stood up and kissed me on the cheek.

Sayana was my first experience with raising a child. I was the one who took her to appointments, was there when she was sick, and everything else big that happened in her life. However, how the hell was I going to juggle raising a two-year-old and having this baby?

❧ 10 ☙

GRIZZ

"**W**hat the fuck do you mean you don't hear a heartbeat?" I barked as the doctor moved the machine around.

"You're saying you're around six weeks, but you're measuring around four weeks. I see a baby, but the heartbeat isn't there, which leaves me to believe that you miscarried. You just didn't pass the baby. We're going to have to remove the baby surgically, so I'm going to admit you to the hospital."

"My man, you missing what the fuck I'm saying." I raised my voice again. He was nervous as hell, and me hovering over him wasn't helping none.

"My baby is gone?" Sundae whispered as she stared at the sonogram like the little jelly bean on the screen was going to move.

"I'm sorry. Yes, you have miscarried. This is common for how early you were." He tried to sympathize and offer some words of wisdom to her. "The nurse will start the process of admitting you to the hospital."

"How long will I be here?" she choked out.

"Two days. Long as everything goes well, you'll be out of here by then." He gave a straight smile and closed the door behind him.

There was nothing except silence that engulfed the room. If I dropped a piece of lint, you could probably hear the shit hit the floor. I tried to touch her, and she stopped my hand and sat up on the table. Wiping her tears away, she looked at me and then looked away. There was hurt, disappointment, and anger written all over her face. I didn't know if she wanted to cry, scream, or hit me. If that's what it took for her to feel better, then I was down with her doing it. I felt like shit because she miscarried the baby. Part of me felt like this shit was my fault because of all the stress I was causing. While this was supposed to be the happiest time in our life, she was living with her friend while I continued to sleep in a hotel. Teyanna didn't suspect a thing, and that shit was crazy. Here me and my woman were, sleeping under other roofs instead of the one I bought us. Sundae couldn't be excited about her pregnancy because she was going through it with me.

"Baby, I lost our baby too." I broke our silence, and she looked at me with disgust written all over her face.

"This isn't about you, Grizz. It has never been just about you. All the shit that has been happening has been happening to me. The one thin..." Her voice broke. "The one thing that brought me a piece of happiness was taken away from me. You want to sit here and gain sympathy from me? Baby boy, you got better luck getting you a cat to love because if it wasn't clear before, we're done," she told me, and each word she said broke my heart just a bit more. The way she spoke and looked at me when she spoke told me everything that I needed to know.

"I'm fucking sorry. How many more times do you want me to tell you? I fucked up, and I blame it on my heart, man."

"Nah, don't put the blame on your heart. It's true you have a big heart, but you had the signs in your face and refused to see it for what it was. I'm not blaming you for having a big heart, I'm blaming you because you're a damn dummy. That baby is gone, and we have no connection to each other. You can leave."

"I'm not goi—"

"That wasn't an option. You can leave. And if you don't, I'll scream that you slapped me for losing your baby. Either leave willingly or by force by the cops," she threatened, her voice dripped with coldness.

"Yo, you would do that shit to me?"

"Just like you allowed a bitch to come into our lives and paint me out to be a crazy bitch? Damn skippy."

The nurse entered the room and looked at both of us. "Should I come back?"

"No, you're fine. He was just leaving," she replied.

"I love you, Sundae."

"And I love food. Get the fuck on," she spat.

I looked at her once more before I left the room. This shit was worse than I fucking thought. At first, I thought that we needed some space and then we would come back together. It seemed like Sundae got rid of that thought and wanted things to be ended forever. That wasn't something I was willing or ready to accept. I fought so hard to have her, and I'd be damned if I lost her because of fucking Teyanna's conniving ass. As I exited the hospital building, I called Manic. Like I knew he would, he answered right away.

"Yerrrrrr!" his loud ass answered. It didn't matter the time of day, he always fucking answered the phone like that.

"Meet me for drinks," I told him.

"Done. Text me the place," he replied and ended the call. There was no explanation or anything; he was always there for me when I needed him. I never had to tell him reasons or make excuses. When I needed him, he always came running for me, just like I would do for him.

I quickly googled some bars and then found one and sent him a message with the address to the bar. This shit had me feeling like I was about to have a heart attack or something. My damn chest was tight as hell, and I knew it had to be because of Sundae. She had a nigga down here hurt as fuck about how she treated me. I was a nigga that sent bitches to the left, but with Sundae, it was different. She wasn't just any bitch; she was wifey, and I did her wrong. She trusted me, and in return, I didn't trust her. When she needed me to trust her, I tossed out accusations and accused her of shit that didn't sound like her. When she needed me the most, I was nowhere to be found, and that shit hurt me like hell, knowing that my woman needed me, and I was with my ex, trying to help her get better. That shit hit a nigga like a ton of bricks. Then, if all that shit wasn't enough, I had to be told that she miscarried. It seemed like bad news loved me because I was always getting the shit.

It was a hipster bar that I found. I didn't give a fuck about the vibe or the patrons inside the damn bar. Long as they could serve me a drink on the rocks, I was cool. I found a space at the bar toward the end and held the seat for Manic. He told me he was about ten minutes away, so I ordered a drink in the meantime. Life was hitting me hard as hell because Jah was up, and I hadn't been by there to see him yet. Sooner or later, I needed to bite the bullet and go up there to see him. I think him getting shot fucked with me the most because I usually did the pickups with him. Once he started walking again, he told me that he was cool and could do them alone. Still, I should have been there with him.

"What's good? You got me in this weirdo ass bar in the middle of the day... You good?" Manic hit me on the back and took a seat beside me.

"Sundae lost the baby," I revealed.

"Shit... My bad, nigga. I'm sorry." He apologized and squeezed my shoulder. "You sure these chicks not getting abortions? 'Cause Remi's ass had one not too long ago, then Tweeti had one, and now Sundae. They all friends... just think about it." Leave it to this nigga to make a joke out of something. Even with how shitty I was feeling, I laughed.

"You stupid."

"You laughing, but I'm serious as hell. Let Paisley come up with some shit like that... beating that girl's ass."

"Nah, the baby is still inside her. That's why she thought she was still pregnant," I explained to him, and he nodded.

"Damn, you and Sundae can't catch a damn break. First the shit with Teyanna, and now this shit. Are y'all even gonna recover from this shit? 'Cause, nigga."

"She told me we're done."

"Yeah, Paisley tried telling me that shit." He waved over for a drink.

"And what happened?"

"I ended up in her bed that same night. The hell she mean we're over? This shit is for life. Soon as I shot up her club, we're forever."

"Shot up her club?"

"Nutted inside her," he clarified, and I shook my head. This nigga was truly a fucking maniac. The crazy shit was that he made no apologies for the crazy shit he did.

"If she said it's over, then, nigga, you got to respect that."

"Yeah, fuck you and her with that shit. Bet I been up at her crib every night this week. Check this, she trying to pay me rent and shit."

"I think that's good. It allows her to have some independence, and looking at your crazy ass, she may need just that."

"Her job is to cook my damn baby, and that's it. She working for some publishing company and think she legit.

Caught her ass wearing a whole suit up top and had on fucking pajamas at the bottom during a conference call." He held onto the bar and fell out laughing. "When she starts giving me money for the crib, I'm gonna put it in the baby's account."

"Smart. Paisley is a good woman. Don't fuck that shit up, man."

"She getting tired of the shit with Nisha. I could tell this time she let me rock with not breaking up, but I can tell the next time she gonna step."

"What's going on with Nisha?"

"She just being extra as fuck. This gender reveal is coming up, and she being all extra and shit. She sent both me and Paisley an invitation to the reveal."

"Oh hell, she bold as fuck." I laughed. Nisha had always been one to be petty. She was in love with Manic, and knowing that Paisley had him, she couldn't allow that to happen. Long as she continued to get under Paisley's skin and cause problem in their relationship, she was going to continue to keep doing the shit.

"Yeah, and Paisley talking about she's going too."

"Shit, Paisley bold too." I laughed. Talking about all his problems had a way of making me forget all about mine for the moment.

"They both crazy as fuck. All I want is two healthy babies. Let my babies come out all skinny and shit, and I'm slapping both of them for stressing my babies out."

"You stupid."

"You handled Teyanna?"

I guzzled my second drink and shook my head. "Nah."

"Nigga, you young, dumb, or full of cum?"

"Don't you ever say some homo shit like that to me again," I threatened him and motioned for the bartender to bring me another drink.

"Why the fuck isn't she pushing up roses? She look like a rose kind of girl."

"Because I haven't had the heart to go over there and handle the shit yet. Every time I go and do it, I end up backing out or making excuses."

"This woman lied and fucked up the happy home you had. You finally had that piece of happiness we've been wanting since kids, and she came and fucked that shit up for you. She snatched that shit away like Baby Dee snatched those cupcakes off the hood of Craig's car. You let this bitch enter your life for the second time and snatch something that means more to you than money. You gonna let her do that shit?" he questioned and looked at his phone. "Shit. Paisley has an appointment tonight. She lucky the doctor allowed it. She already pissing me off with her little job. You good?"

"Yeah. I'm straight. Tell Paisley I said what's good." I dapped him, and he headed out the bar. "I got his tab," I told the bartender. That nigga was acting like he was about to chase him or something.

I continued to sit there, and the words that Manic told me kept ringing through my head. She took my money years ago and dipped out. Now she was back and had managed to fuck up the one thing that meant the world to me. The question was, was I going to let her get away with it?

SOMETIME AROUND TWO IN THE MORNING, I PULLED INTO the driveway of my home. It almost felt foreign because I didn't see Sundae's car in the driveway. I was buzzed from all my drinks, but not that buzzed where I couldn't drive or my find my way home. I pushed my key through the door, and the alarm blared. I hit the code and then continued into the kitchen. It was spotless, not a crumb in sight. The house smelled like vanilla, and I cringed. Sundae couldn't stand the fragrance vanilla, and this bitch had my whole house lit up.

"Grizz? You had me ready to call the cops on you." Teyanna switched the light on. She had on a silk green robe and her hair was in a bonnet. When she saw me staring, she snatched it off, and her long hair fell out the bonnet.

"The chemo don't make your hair fall out?"

"Huh?"

"Your hair... how you still have all that damn hair with you doing treatments."

"Each patient is different. You hungry? I made some oxtails earlier." She switched the subject.

"Yeah."

She came in the kitchen and pulled out the plastic bowls and got to heating me up some food. I leaned against the wall and watched as she moved around the kitchen like the shit was hers. "What you been up to? You or Sundae haven't been here. It's been hard trying to care for myself by myself."

"Shit with me and Sundae been hard, so we been trying to work on it."

Teyanna turned around quick and stared at me like I was crazy. "Work on it? She's nuts, and you're trying to work on being with her?" I could tell the subject pissed her off.

"Yeah, that's gonna be my wife. I want to marry that woman."

"Marry her? Grizz, I know she may have some good pussy or something, but you want to marry the crazy bitch?" I wanted to slap the taste out her mouth, but I continued to fuck with her head a little further.

"Sundae been nothing but nice to you. Why you hating on her?" I questioned. This woman had serious hate penned up against Sundae, and all Sundae had ever been was good to her fake ass.

"That bitch walks around here like she's the queen and

I'm beneath her. She's never wanted me here, and you know that." I waved her off and went upstairs to grab some cash out my safe. Having drinks at that expensive bar had me low on cash. Teyanna abandoned what she was doing downstairs and followed right behind me. "Grizz, I'm still in love with you. I want to be the only woman in your life. You don't need a mentally weak bitch in your corner; you need me."

"You got fucking cancer, Teyanna. You're equally fucking weak." I kicked my boots off and plopped down on the foot of my bed.

"I lied, Grizz. I don't have cancer." She admitted what I wanted her to admit. "I just wanted you to give me a second chance. I thought by me acting sick, we would grow closer, but Sundae kept getting in the fucking way, so I had to find a way to push you two apart so me and you could work." She bent down between my legs and stared up at me. She was rubbing my thighs and looking at me with this pathetic ass look on her face.

"So you lied about being sick? What the fuck else you did to get me back?" I was calm when I spoke because it was one thing knowing it ahead of time, but it was another thing hearing the bitch admit to the role she played in fucking my life up.

"I messed around with Sundae's pills. At first, I was second guessing, but the more the bitch walked around, the more she pissed me off. I decided to mess with her pills and let you see the real her. You saw how nasty she was to us, baby. You're better off without her." She started to inch her hand closer to my dick.

"You telling me that you did all this shit so we can be together? Sundae just miscarried our baby because of all the fucking stress you have caused. Are we any closer to being together?"

Teyanna screwed her face up. "She didn't need to have a

fucking baby by you. So the baby can come out as crazy as she is? It was God's pla—" I snapped. I grabbed 'hold of her neck with both of my hands and squeezed. She was gasping for air and scratching at me. "I... can't... bre..." She lost her voice, and I continued to choke her out.

"Bitch, you took everything away from me, thinking I would ever be with you. I took you in my home out the kindness of my own heart, and you try to end my girl and fuck up what we had. I fucking trusted the shit out of you, and that was my fucking fault," I said through gritted teeth. I realized that she was no longer scratching, and her eyes were rolled to the back of her head. I let go of her neck, and she fell back onto the floor.

I felt her neck and checked for a pulse, and I had killed her. Killing her felt good. Wrapping my hands around her neck while I felt her fight for air felt like I won a million dollars. I came into the crib and had the mind to tell her I knew about everything and was giving her the option to flee and never come the fuck back. The more she spoke about the shit she did to tear my life apart for her own selfish needs, the angrier I became. She spoke like the shit was cool and that she was allowed to come into my life and decide if Sundae was good for me or not. The fact that I trusted a bitch that was untrustworthy told me that I needed to stop fucking thinking with my heart. The only woman that meant anything to me was done with me because of the shit that I allowed to happen. I allowed Teyanna to come into my crib and have Sundae looking like a fucking fool. I should have never allowed that bitch to cross the threshold of our home. I stood to my feet and paced the floor and then grabbed my phone.

"Clean up," was all I said when the person on the other side of the line answered. I ended the phone, tossed the phone onto my bed, and went to take a shower. It was time to reclaim my damn life, and now that this bitch was gone, I needed to work on getting my woman back.

❧ 11 ❧

UZI

"Here you go running off again while we're trying to discuss our life," Remi complained as I pulled on my jeans.

I had got a call from one of my cops I paid on the force. He told me that he had some information for me about some cop he overheard talking about me to their sergeant. Shit like that couldn't wait while I sat here and spoke to Remi about why she didn't want to have fucking kids. In my opinion, even if I didn't have to run out, this conversation was pissing me off.

"What are we discussing? The fact that you don't want to have kids? There's not much to fucking discuss."

"Why are you acting like we can't be happy without having kids of our own? We have Paris. Shouldn't that be enough?" she whined and looked at me with sad eyes.

"Paris is about to be fucking grown. She's applying for college and shit, and you want me to be okay with never having any more kids? I get what you went through fucked you up mentally, but for you to decide something that involves both of us is fucked up."

"How? I don't want to have any kids, and you and everybody else have been pushing it on me. I don't want to have any kids, and I'm fine with that. We don't need kids to be happy," she tried to convince me, and I pulled my boots on.

"Yeah, *you* don't need kids to be happy. I want fucking kids, and you over here acting like I'm wrong for that. Paris was born, and I wasn't there like I should have been. She's older now, and I'm ready to have a son or a daughter with the woman that's about to be my wife."

Remi rolled her eyes and got up from the bed. I could tell she was pissed because the conversation wasn't going the way she wanted it to go. She wanted me to just agree with what she wanted. I didn't want to sit here and tell her that I didn't want to have kids. That shit would have been a lie, and we would have issues down the line. If Remi didn't want to have kids, I didn't think we would make it down the aisle.

"I'm sick of sacrificing shit because of you and what your family wants. Your mom always mentions when we're going to try again, and I'm sick of it."

"Yeah, what the fuck ever, Remi. It was no wonder that I got you pregnant."

"I wish it never happened. I finally got you not talking about the baby we aborted and then this happened," she mumbled, but I heard her loud and clear. "Maybe we don't need to get married," she blurted and turned toward me.

"I was thinking the same thing." From her expression, I could tell she wasn't expecting me to say what I had said to her.

"The wedding is off." She whimpered and went into the bathroom. Her yelling and venting were followed by the door slamming.

I grabbed my phone, money, and headed downstairs. Paris was texting and eating breakfast when I went into the kitchen. "Hey, Daddy." I bent down and kissed her on the cheek. She had this little boy that she was friends with, so I was watching her ass like a hawk.

"What you doing today?"

"Shopping and coming home to watch movies with Remi." She shrugged. All her ass did was shop. "My mom is supposed to visit next week."

"She bringing your sister?"

"Nope. She said it's a getaway from my sister. I guess her and Uncle are going to do something while away from the baby."

"Let me get this straight. You haven't seen your little sister in a while, and she doesn't bring her so you can see her?"

"It's Mom, Daddy. Are you really surprised?"

"Nah. Look, I have to make some runs, so I'll be home later. You went up there to see your uncle yet?"

"Yep. Yesterday, and he said I was dressed like a baby prostitute." She giggled. "I told him to shut up before I pulled the plug on his ass."

"Aye, language."

"Sorry. He seems to be back to his old self, except he stuttered a bit."

"Yeah, if that's the only damage he took from a shot in the head, I'll take it. Behave yourself, and don't be spending all my damn money in those malls with your friends," I warned and left out the house.

Remi had me all mad, and I knew the rest of the day was going to be left to shit. Business had to be handled, and I needed to make sure whoever thought they could fuck with my family was going to be dealt with. I hopped in my whip and headed up to the hospital to kick it with Jah. The detective was going to meet me up at the hospital. As I was driving, my phone started ringing. Reaching down, I picked up the phone and put it on speaker.

"And then you're going to leave and not say anything to me. I'm glad the wedding is off. This relationship has been fucking draining!" Remi yelled through the phone. She couldn't take that I left the situation alone. She always had to have the last word.

"Draining? When was it draining? When I had you all around the world traveling and shopping? Or was it when I was fucking making sure you never had to work a day in your life again?"

"Now you're throwing everything up in my face? I wanted to travel and have fun before settling down. I wanted to be married and have fun, not be settled down with a baby and you always gone. You see what the hell Tweeti putting up with. Soon as she had that baby, Jah was over there cheating on her."

"Bye, Remi." I ended the call with her. She was trying to find any and everything to use as an excuse when the problem was her.

She more than anything knew that Jah never cheated on Tweeti, yet she still wanted to use that as an excuse. Right now, I couldn't have her occupying any more of my damn head space with this shit. If she didn't want to have kids, that was a fucking deal breaker for me. I had one daughter, and I loved having kids. More kids were always in the plan for me, not with Paris's hoe ass mama, but eventually with my future wife. Knowing that my future wife didn't want to have kids had me fucked up.

It didn't take me long to get to the hospital and head upstairs. I was glad they moved him out that damn CCU unit. I was getting tired of paying that woman extra money to have more people come up there. When I walked into the room, Grizz and Manic was up there with Jah. I dapped them and then went to go dap my brother.

"How you feeling, playa?"

"Here and there." He laughed. "Damn throat still feels like it's on fire," he complained.

"They giving you something for it? You need me to raise hell in here?"

"Chill. They treating me better than most. That medicine not working, but Tweet bringing me some throat drops later," he explained.

"Where is your little pit bull? You know she banned all of us from seeing you when you first got shot? She still on my shit list."

"What y'all did to my baby? She only cut y'all off when you get on her nerves and shit." He took up for his wife like I knew he would. Tweeti and Jah's shit was iron clad. They both would defend each other to the end of the world. Nobody couldn't say shit without the other one jumping down the person's throat.

"Yeah, whatever. You finally found your way up here?" I nudged Grizz as I sat down. He seemed different. I didn't know; the nigga seemed like he was high or something. "You high?"

"He had to smoke him a big one after fucking killing Teyanna's ass." Manic said it like it wasn't nothing.

"You fucking with me? How'd you do it?" I needed fucking details. The way shorty came into he and Sundae's life and fucked shit up, I needed to know how he took her ass out this world.

"I ain't even plan on doing shit to her. Was gonna give her some bread and tell her to leave town or something," he admitted, and we all looked at his ass like he was stupid.

"Nigga, that's why Sundae not fucking with yo' ass now." Manic was the first to speak out of all of us.

"Hell yeah. You wild for even considering that. I got one bitch I want to take out, and if I wasn't in this hospital, she'd be dead." Jah pointed his IV ridden arm at Grizz.

"You letting Dakota still live in that apartment is hilarious. I would have been had that bitch thrown the fuck out of my shit," Manic said.

"Nah. I have a plan for her ass, and if I kick her out, then she gonna know something," he responded.

"Y'all heard about your boy Rome?" Grizz brought up.

"Yeah, the nigga dead. Who the fuck cares?" Manic put his foot up on the chair next to him.

"Nah, did you hear who did this shit?" Grizz continued to hint.

"Who?" I didn't give a fuck about Rome dying. That nigga was a little fish compared to what the fuck I was dealing with. I did want to know how the fuck he got killed and who did the shit.

"Tweek," Grizz revealed. We all turned to look at him like he was crazy. Tweek and Rome were like fucking brothers. He wouldn't kill his brother, and if he did, what the fuck for?

"Tweek is his fucking brother. Why the fuck would he do that?" Jah took the words right out of my mouth.

"He was fucking his fiancée." Manic laughed. "Nigga was digging his damn brother's fiancée out and got the karma he deserved. Now, his baby mama getting killed was fucked up, but she already knew that was a part of the life that Rome lived."

"Nigga, you knew this whole time?" Grizz looked at Manic.

"Hell yeah. The day he got killed, his baby mama's mom called Paisley. And guess what? She's now the guardian of his fucking daughter who keeps crying every damn night for her mama that was never there!" Manic roared.

"Can you please keep it down," one of the nurses said and closed the door behind her. Jah burst out laughing as he sipped his water.

"Damn, this nigga had more information than I did,"

Grizz joked. "You spoke to Tweek too?"

"Hell nah. You did?"

"Yeah, he hit me a few days ago and told me to meet him. I met up with him for a drink or six, and he told me he cut the nigga's brakes. He and Syria were street racing up in Delaware with some niggas, and boom, they couldn't stop."

"Oh, that nigga Tweek is cold as fuck," I admitted. Tweek and Rome were known for always betting money street racing. A few times, Tweek tried to convince me to expand into street racing, and I turned him down because of it. That shit was too risky and too hot for what I was doing. He and Rome did it as an illegal hobby, and the shit killed both him and his baby mama. I felt bad for his daughter; growing up without both her parents was going to be hard.

"Word. He still with his shorty?" Jah quizzed.

"Hell yeah. He's not going to leave her ass. Especially after he just killed over her. That nigga crazy over her. After speaking to the nigga, I noticed he has a few screws loose or something," Grizz said.

"Ya think? The nigga did some shit that I would do. Let Paisley do some shit like that, and I'm fucking popping her. She ain't gonna leave me out here being a single father. Hell nah.'"

"You hear this nigga?" I looked at Grizz and Jah. "You really fucking crazy. How the fuck you gonna blame her for being a single father when you gonna kill her."

"Don't matter. She shouldn't have been out here fucking and sucking." Manic waved me off and looked toward the door.

"I'm interrupting, fellas?" Detective Orr walked into the room.

"I swear I can't stand your ass. Why the fuck you up here now?" Manic stood up and gave him the free seats and went to sit in the window.

"Mitchell, you and I have a love hate relationship." Detective Orr sighed and sat down in the seats that Manic was just sitting in.

"You wild, Manic." I laughed. It didn't matter how many cops we had on payroll, he still couldn't stand they asses. "What you got for me, Orr?"

"Jordan Barron ring a bell to you?"

I checked my mental rolodex and thought of the name. It wasn't like the name was some unique name. I probably ran across a bunch of fucking Jordans during the years. How the hell was I supposed to fucking know if it rang a bell?

"Should it?"

"You killed his brother a while back... and his mother," he refreshed my memory.

"Ah, I know who you talking about, but his name wasn't fucking Jordan."

"His older brother, who is a cop on the force, name is Jordan. I overheard your name come up when I walked passed the sergeant's office and he was in there. I work damn hard to make sure the McKnight name is never mentioned around my department."

"So then why the fuck is my brother's name being mentioned?" Jah interrupted.

"Because apparently, this man is in his feelings because you killed his little brother and his mother," Detective Orr explained.

"I mean, shit, I would be in my feelings too. You fucking monster, Uzi." Manic's crazy ass laughed like the shit was funny.

"What the fuck your boss say?" I was more concerned with if his fucking boss was going to investigate us. The last time that shit happened, it cost me out the ass to make the shit go away. I wasn't prepared to pay millions to make a bunch of crooked cops look the other way. Hell, I was already paying them enough if you asked me.

"He told me to check you out and come back to him. The new guy needs to go. Don't know or care how you're going to do it, but get it done. If he fucks up me putting my daughter through college and my son through medical school, there will be a problem."

Orr was only concerned with one person and that was himself. He didn't give a fuck about putting his kids through college or medical school. Orr cared about his little tricking he did with all these hood chicks in the hood. He loved black women and loved to spend more money on them than his wife.

"See what I mean? These muthafuckas be doing shit like this and then want to stand behind the head nigga in charge on the news acting like they the good guys when they arrest niggas like us." Manic jumped down from the window and pointed to Detective Orr. This nigga really hated the cops, and it was the same charade whenever we had to meet with one of them.

Orr stood up and fixed his suit jacket and headed toward the door. "If you would just let me lock his ass up, we wouldn't have to do this every time. Like I said, fix this issue. He works the precinct in the mornings before going out on patrol. Fellas." He waved and left the room as quick as he came.

Detective Orr never stayed around long. If I started fucking with his money, then I would see him a lot more. "We need to get this shit solved now. If it ain't one thing it's a fucking 'nother." Jah slapped his hands on his legs.

"Nigga, you really need to chill before your legs fall off. I heard you got shot in them shits, and you over here slapping them and shit," Manic chimed in.

Ignoring Manic, I turned to Grizz. "I want you and Manic

on this shit. Pick his ass up and bring him to the same warehouse we killed his moms and brother in. Nigga think he gonna fuck with me and get away with the shit, he dead wrong."

"Bet. But we can scoop his ass whenever he gets off. Don't pigs usually patrol in their barn car togeth—"

"Manic, we get you don't like cops. Damn." Jah cut him off. "You think he was the one who took the shots at me?"

"Nah, too risky of a cop," I replied.

"It do make sense. You took his brother out, and he was trying to do the same to you." Grizz snapped his fingers.

"Yeah, you right. Grab his fucking ass." I gave the final word.

Grizz and Manic got up and dapped both me and Jah and headed out. They had their assignment, and they knew it needed to be done now. This nigga tried to off my brother, and he had to meet his maker. Nobody tried to end a McKnight and lived to speak about the shit. I ended my own half-brother for trying to kill Remi. What the fuck you think I would do to somebody who tried to kill Jahquel?

After Grizz and Manic left, I sat there and looked out the window. "What's wrong?" Jah broke me from my thoughts.

"Nothing, I'm good."

"Nah, I can tell from that stank ass face that something is wrong. Pull your chair over here." He pointed to the empty spot next to his bed.

"When the hell your wife coming back? I'm not in the mood for her shit today." Me and Tweeti still hadn't spoken about what went down. Instead, she said little smart shit whenever we were in the same room.

"Don't worry about her. She's with Sundae, chilling for the day."

"Ight."

"Tell me what the fuck is good with you?"

"Remi don't want to have kids. She told me this morning before I left to come here. She talking about we don't need kids to be happy."

Jah chuckled. "You really don't though."

"Yeah, that's true if you're someone who doesn't want to have kids. Paris is my fucking life, and I can't see myself not having another little me running around."

"Remi just needs some time. She lost the baby, and she's probably having second thoughts about shit. Give her some time to figure out if that's what she wants to do or not. Don't push her into the shit."

"I understand she needs time to heal and deal with it. Jah, she's talking about never. Like she don't ever want to have kids. A life of traveling around the world with my wife is cool and shit, but when we're done, what's next? I'm too old to be sitting here playing the waiting game. She has more time because she's young, but I don't have that time."

"The hell you talking about? We can make babies until we're a hundred years old. Have fun with your woman and then get her drunk and trap her ass."

"The hell? I want my shorty to want my seed. That's how all that postpartum depression shit starts. I want my wife to want our baby."

"She can want the baby and still struggle with that. I think Tweeti struggled with it a bit when Taz was younger."

"Word?"

"Yeah. That was around the time I had to pull away and be there for my wife. I don't know how it feels to go through it, but I just wanted to be there for her and my seed."

"That's love." I nodded.

"On the real, just give her some time and see if she comes around. If not, I don't know what the fuck to tell you. I do know, don't walk down that aisle unless you both have come to an agreement. Marriage is serious."

"Look at me being schooled by my little brother... Enough about these damn women. What's going on with you?"

"My head is healing up. They keep doing all these scans and shit. As far as me walking again, they said it's going to be a long road. I'm 'bout to say fuck this walking shit."

"Man, you was walking, so it can happen again. This is a minor setback for a major comeback. When they releasing you out of here?"

"I don't know. They don't want to release me too early and something happens, so they gonna keep checking me and shit. The doctor keeps telling me how blessed I am to be alive."

"Nigga, that's because you are. We all thought you were gonna die. Shit had us all fucked up, especially Tweeti. I think she took the shit the worse."

"Yeah, that's my baby. After I kill Dakota's ass, I'm gonna make her the happiest woman in the world." He smirked and rubbed his hands together. "It's been a minute, and I can't wait to fuck the shit out of her."

"Aye, too much information." Zuri stepped into the room. She was dressed in a white pantsuit and blue Louboutin heels. "Sorry I couldn't make it the other day," she apologized.

"Nah, you good. Tweeti figured you got busy with the girls," Jah answered.

"Zena has some stomach bug and gave it to her sister," she explained. "How are you feeling? Never mind. I could hear your mouth down the hall, so that already told me something."

"A nigga is back and better. How's my girls?"

She dug into her purse and pulled out some papers. "They made you some stuff. Somebody didn't answer their phone to update me. I had to find out from people."

"Shit, I was busy," I responded. She wasn't going to make me feel bad about not answering her calls. Hell, I didn't even know she and Jah had made up and were even on this level with each other. The last time we were in the same room, these two were damn near fucking growling at each other. I think Jah said some shit about wanting to fucking shoot her ass in the head and hide her body. I stood up and gave Zuri my seat. "I'm 'bout to head out... I'll holla at you later, nigga."

"Bet." He dapped me and I left. Going home was the last thing I planned on doing right now. Remi wasn't ready to talk, and I wasn't about to do that yelling shit. Right now, I was about to go find a bar and drink until it was time to head home.

I WALKED INTO THE WAREHOUSE AT THREE IN THE morning. It seemed like everybody loved to wake me the fuck up at this time. I was tired as fuck, but when Grizz told me that it was urgent, I climbed out of the hotel bed and headed over. Remi was still in her feelings, and when I tried to go home, she had Paris meet me at the door with my Louis Vuitton duffle already packed. Low key, I was happy that I didn't have to deal with her or talk about the situation we were dealing with right now. There were some hard ass decisions that needed to be made. This wasn't something like she loved pancakes and I hated pancakes. This shit was on how we planned to grow our family through the years. If she didn't want to grow our family and I did, then there were some major decisions that needed to be made in our relationship.

"About damn time," Manic said as he sat down at the table in my chair. He stood up and walked over to the nigga with the pillowcase over his head.

"You both work fast." I nodded at both of them. The reason I kept them on my team was because they were so good. Come to think about it, Grizz was put on by Qua. He was his cousin or some shit. The fact that this man stood by my side and was loyal as fuck spoke volumes. He was a part of the family. Then he bought Manic's crazy ass on, and his ass was like the brother who you never wanted but loved because he always said funny shit at the wrong time.

"You don't fuck with one of our own and think you can get away with it." Manic mushed Jordan's head.

I walked over to him and pulled the pillowcase off his head. "You thought you could fuck with my brother and get away with the shit? You know who the fuck I am?"

Manic snatched the duct tape off his mouth. "I'm a fucking cop. You think you're going to get away with this shit?"

"Oh, this nigga got a mouth on him. Who the fuck you think gave your dumb ass up? Now, let me ask... What the fuck were you thinking on accomplishing?"

"You took my family, and I planned on taking yours. You know that fine ass fat bitch you call a sister-in-law? Well, that bitch had community service at my aunt's center, and I planned on starting with her first. I almost had her, but shorty was still wrapped up in her cripple ass husband. I had to ditch that plan. I zeroed in on you and you only. The only way to touch you is with the police, and I planned on having them crash your whole shit down."

"And where did my brother play into this?"

"What the fuck about him?"

"You shooting him in the head." Manic mushed him in the head again. "The fuck you do that for?"

"I didn't fucking touch your brother, although I should have. I should have shot him right between the fucking eyes." He spoke with so much hate. Spit flew out his mouth and landed at my shoe.

I pulled my hand back and punched him right in his shit three times. He spit out blood and looked up at me. "Fuck you and the McKnight family. You took my brother and my mama away from me."

"I did you a fucking favor. Your brother was gonna get himself killed, and your mama should have been swallowed with her crack head ass!" I yelled and went over to the table where Grizz had a gun waiting for me.

"And I was returning the favor when I took down your entire empire. Starting with your little bitch of a fiancée!" he continued to spew his hate.

Cocking the gun back, I aimed it at his head. "This is for my brother." I shot him in the head.

I cocked it back again and shot him in both legs. Just how he did my brother, I did his fuck boy ass. I shot him a few extra times in the head to make sure he was dead. After seeing Jah live after being shot in the head, I was leery that this nigga could still be alive. All that torture shit wasn't for me. Back in the day, I used to live for that shit, but as I got older, that shit got weak. Why the fuck did it matter how the fuck I killed them? It wasn't like they were gonna be in hell bragging about how their lives were ended. When I was younger, there was a bunch of shit I used to love to do that now I didn't even think of doing. All I wanted to do was make sure I got the nigga responsible for trying to take my brother's life. Did I think it was going to be the brother of the little nigga I took out? Nah, that didn't cross my path not once. Now that the shit was done, I knew I would be able to get a good night's sleep tonight.

"Clean this shit up. I'll holla at y'all another time. Good looks."

"You already know," Grizz said and dapped me. I went to the back and switched clothes and headed back out just like I came. It took longer than I wanted, but the nigga who tried to kill my brother was dead, and I was the one who killed him.

❧ 12 ❧

SUNDAE

Losing the baby felt like I lost my soul. Just like I was for her, Tweeti was there for me through every step of the way. Soon as I kicked Grizz out the hospital room, she was the first person I called. I needed somebody to be there and hold my hand, and she was there like I needed. Grizz should have been there, but I couldn't stand seeing his face any longer. Each time I saw his face, it reminded me of all the shit he did to me. It reminded me that he was the one who put us through everything we were going through. This was supposed to be a happy time in our lives. We were supposed to be expecting a baby, working toward marriage, and living life like we were. Then Teyanna entered our lives and tore the whole thing upside down. It was hard trying to move on when you were still in love. As mad as Grizz made me, I loved the shit out him and didn't think I would be able to stop.

"Girl, get out of your head." Tweeti tossed a t-shirt at my head. I was laid across she and Jah's bed in my own little world.

"You dragged me out the house, and now you're bothering me... What more do you want from me, woman?"

"You been in that house with Paisley too long. All that child do is sit in the house, and now that she has that little girl, that's really all she does."

"Sayana is sweet. It's sad what happened to her parents, but she's a sweet little girl. When she first came, she cried all night long for her mother."

"Whew, chile... How did you deal with it?" Tweeti laughed and put more stuff into the bag she was packing for Jah. They were allowing him to get out that hospital gown, so he had Tweeti bringing him some clothes so she could wash him.

"I was sitting in the kitchen at the counter while she paced back and forth and soothed her. We even took turns until she fell asleep. The next morning, we woke up in Paisley's bed tired as hell." I laughed.

Sayana was so cute when she wasn't crying and screaming. Paisley had so much patience with her and cared so much for that little girl. You could tell from how she sang to her before she put her down for bed. I told her a million times that she was going to be a great mother. Paisley was so different when she was in mommy mode as I liked to call it. She had this glow to her as if the angels were shining their light on her.

"You both are hilarious. All you need to do is give her a bottle and lay her butt down. How old is she?"

"I think she just turned two or something."

"I still can't believe that Rome and his baby mama died. Paisley is good, because I would have had that little girl in foster care."

"Tweet, no you wouldn't."

"Try me. Didn't he have that little girl during their relationship? Paisley is too nice, and that man found a way to have a hold on her even from the grave."

"Tweet, she loves that little girl. It's kind of like her daughter in a way."

"*Like* a daughter. She didn't have that little girl. Anyway, I'm glad you are settling at her place and have decided to stay long term."

"Being at your house and riding past the house I shared with Grizz is so weird to me. I miss my home." I sighed.

I hated being stuck in that house at first, and now there were things that I missed about it. I missed my deep soaking tub or the wall I used to scratch my lower back on when nobody was around to scratch it for me. It was shit about that house that I missed and loved. Except, every time I thought about my beautiful home, I thought about Teyanna walking her ass through the door and fucking up life as I knew it.

"Are you really done with Grizz? And before you open your mouth, just remember that it's just me and you," Tweeti reminded me.

"We're done."

"So you ready to walk away from him for good? That man was there for you even when I wasn't."

"And that man wasn't there for me when you were. I wasn't myself, and he never noticed. Instead, he continued to place the blame on me for a bitch that turned out to be his ex-girlfriend... Right now, I'm over him."

"Right now? So there's hope for this?"

"None at all. I'm done as of right now."

"You see when you use words like *right now* or *as of right now*, you know that doesn't make me believe you."

"Who knows what the future holds. Right now, I'm over him and every other nigga that tries to kick it to me. I want to focus on myself and my mental health. I can't keep putting people and shit ahead of me. I need to focus on me right now."

"I agree. And how do you feel about losing the baby?"

I leaned up on the bed and shrugged my shoulders. "I'm sad about it. Then, I think what if right now wasn't the right time for it anyway? I'm sure God will bless me with a baby in the future. And I hope he does it when my life is less chaotic and I'm not being a roommate to a pregnant girl and a toddler."

"It will happen for you and Remi both," she told me and plopped down on the bed beside me. "Hand me my phone." I passed her the phone and she checked her messages.

"I'm just saying, I'—"

"What the fuck? Come take a ride with me. My mind has been cleared, and I forgot all about this bitch. Guess what, she about to be handled today!" Tweeti yelled and jumped off the bed. I didn't even know what the hell had just happened. One second, I was about to continue talking about my life, and the next, Tweeti was changing her clothes and taking off her jewelry.

"What happened?"

"This bitch in my condo blasting loud music, and the building managers are complaining about it."

"I thought you guys owned it though?"

"We do. Jah was actually about to sell it, but shit happened. Even with owning, you have to abide by the rules in place by management. They left me three voicemails and called like twelve times."

"What are we going to do? You know I'm down."

"We going to move little bitch right on out. I've been itching to do that shit but lost track because of everything with Jah," she said as she grabbed her purse, keys, and my arm to grab me out the house.

Tweeti backed her whip out fast as hell out of her driveway. If I could, I would have wrapped my damn seat belt around me twice with the way Tweeti was driving down her block. We sped past my old house, and all I could do was sigh. I really did miss my house and wished that me and Grizz could make this work. I loved my man more than anything and wanted to make it work with him. Still, part of me couldn't act like what he did, didn't happen. I couldn't ignore the fact that he didn't have trust or faith in me or our relationship. At the end of the day, if me and Grizz were going to be together, it was in God's plan.

With the way Tweeti drove, we made it to Brooklyn in record time. She swung her car in the parking garage and was out the car just as quick as we parked. I had to grab her key fob out the car and chase behind her. I had just managed to catch the elevator just as she was aggressively pressing the button to close it.

"Damn, can you wait a second." I slid into the elevator right next to Tweeti. The elevator door closed and brought us up to their old floor.

"I've been waiting on this bitch," she growled as she rushed down the stairs. Digging in her purse, she grabbed her keys and let us into the apartment.

There were no music playing. In fact, it was quiet as hell when we entered the apartment. Tweeti rushed through the door and dropped her purse onto the counter. Dakota was coming out the backroom when we walked in.

"What the hell are you doing in my home?" the bitch had the nerve to say. She was holding a towel in one hand and shampoo in the other.

"Nah, bitch, I dreamed about this fucking day!" Tweeti yelled and lunged at Dakota. Each time she had lunged at her in that past, there was always someone right there to grab her and stop her from doing something. Well, besides the time when she punched her in the face while she was pregnant.

I watched as Tweeti grabbed the girl by the hair and swung her onto the floor. The blows she threw to this girl's face reminded me of Mike Tyson. She continued to whip her ass throughout the living room while Dakota screamed. It wasn't until I heard baby cries from the back that I decided to step in and pull Tweeti off her.

"And every time I see your ugly dog smelling ass, I'm tagging your ass," Tweeti continued to threaten.

"Chill, her baby is here," I told her.

"I don't give a fuck about her baby. She didn't give a fuck about mine when she tried to ruin my family for some fucking money. Low budget ass bitch!" she hollered and tried to go over there and continue what she had started.

Dakota was on the floor groaning and tried to pick herself up off the floor. "You're going to prison. I'm not dropping the charges this fucking time!" she had the nerve to yell at Tweeti. Did she not know that she was still able to get her ass whipped before the cops came? Shorty was better off keeping her mouth shut. At the end of the day, if Tweeti wanted to get to her, she was going to get to her, and my little ass wasn't going to be able to hold her back.

"Bitch, fucking try. You got twenty minutes to grab you, your baby, and get the fuck out my house. And if you're one second over that twenty minutes, I'm beating your ass with your baby in your hands!" Tweeti screamed and went into the kitchen.

She started tossing shit out the fridge and pouring out baby formula in the sink. When she did that, I stopped her. "Tweet, believe it or not, that baby is innocent. Let her pack him some food and stuff."

"Fuck her and that baby. She tried to use that baby to tear my family apart." Tweeti pulled away from me, and I tried to grab her again. "Get off me, Sundae."

"Tweeti, you don't want to get locked up again. This bitch called the cops," I warned her. She ignored me and headed over to her.

Dakota hovered over in the corner like a scared little cat.

She kept looking at us like we were the damn veterinarian or something. Tweeti grabbed her skinny ass up by her neck and held her against the wall. "Let me make myself clear, bitch. You grab that big-headed ass baby and get the fuck out my condo. Don't come the fuck back for nothing because all of this shit was provided under false pretenses. If I see your face again, I'm tagging your ass again and again until I'm satisfied... you hear me?" Tweeti applied more pressure to her neck where she was gasping.

"Y...Yes." She nodded her head up and down quickly. Tweeti released her, and she fell to the floor like a rag doll.

Tweeti stepped over her and went into the kitchen. She had the nerve to grab a bottle of water out the fridge and guzzle it before tossing the bottle at Dakota's head. I couldn't hold it in, and I started laughing while Tweeti kept this disgusted look on her face. I mean, why wouldn't she? This woman tore her family apart, and she did it for nothing. The baby wasn't Jah's baby, and he had never slept with the woman. Still, she continued to fuck with her family and tear her marriage apart. I think what fucked with Tweeti the most was that she could have lost Jah, and they were on bad terms. She wouldn't have been able to forgive herself if he had died and she never got to tell him she was sorry for not believing him or tell him that she loved him.

"You heard what I said, bitch," Tweeti reminded her as we left out the door. We headed back downstairs. I followed behind Tweeti and shook my head because she wasn't playing. This anger had been brewing since she punched Dakota in the face when she was pregnant. If Dakota was smart, she would get the hell out that condo before she got her ass whipped again.

A BOTTLE OF WINE, SADE, AND THIS COUCH FELT LIKE

everything. Paisley took Sayana to the movies and dinner tonight. She was sick of being in the house with her, so she decided to take her out. My mind was mentally exhausted. Each time I refilled my wine glass, I was back refilling it five minutes after. The wine was taking over my body, and the buzz felt good. I knew I shouldn't have been drinking with my medicine, but I needed an escape. The baby, Grizz, and Teyanna all were on my mind, and I just needed a way not to think of it all for a minute. I was sure the wine mixing with my night meds were the cause of me feeling extra buzzed. Looking around the condo, I sighed. The condo was a nice one and in a good building; still, it wasn't home for me. I appreciated everything Paisley did to make me feel comfortable; however, when I fell asleep at night, all I thought about was the home I shared in Staten Island with Grizz.

A knock at the door deterred me from my thoughts. I looked at the door and sighed because Paisley probably forgot her keys again. "I knew you didn't have your keys." I laughed and staggered to the door.

I pulled the door open and stopped short when I saw Grizz standing there. He stood there towering over me and looking down into my eyes as I looked up into his eyes. "We need to talk," he told me. Not asked but told me that we needed to talk. I wasn't that buzzed, but I could have sworn I told his big ass not to just show up here unannounced.

"*We* don't need to do a damn thing," I slurred.

"You been drinking?"

"Here you go... about to act like poppa bear but couldn't be that when I needed you the most." I rolled my eyes. "Talk, since we need to talk."

"I'm not about to sit out in the hallway and talk about my personal shit. You either let me come in or you come home and talk to me." He gave me two options. Out of the two options he gave me, I didn't want to do either of them. Still, I knew enough time had passed, and we definitely needed to talk.

"Come in." I sighed and held the door open for him. He walked in, and I shut the door behind him. "Want something to drink?"

"I'll take whatever you have?"

"Rat poison cocktail good with you?" I rolled my eyes and went to the fridge and grabbed him a bottle of water.

"For real? How long you gonna keep being mean to me?"

"Until I fucking feel like it." I shoved the water bottle into his chest.

Plopping on the couch across from him, I poured more wine into my empty wine glass. "You know you're not supposed to be drinking."

"You know you're not supposed to be drinking... Nigga, shut up." I rolled my eyes and sipped my drink.

He opened his water bottle and guzzled it in five seconds. I sat back, staring at his fine ass. Why did he have to do some fuck shit to me? All I wanted to do was fuck the shit out of him and then lay in the bed right beside him.

"You gonna talk or just stare at me?" He snapped me from my thoughts.

"You came to my door and asked to talk. I didn't come looking for you." I put my empty glass down on the coffee table and crossed my legs. "What's up? What you need to talk about?"

"Us."

"What about us?"

"Baby, I'm fucking sorry for the shit I did to you. I was blinded, and I shouldn't have did you that way. Teyanna had me thinking she was really dying, and I just wanted to help her out. If I would have known that she was up to that fuck shit, I would have ended her right then and there." He apologized like he did each time I'd seen him.

"Do you really know what you did? 'Cause you've been apologizing, but do you even know what you're apologizing for?" Grizz thought the problem was Teyanna, and she was a part of the problem; she just wasn't the main problem.

"Explain it to me. I want to know what I did so I can fix this... so I can fix us," he pleaded and leaned up in the chair. The sad thing was that I could tell he was genuinely sorry for what he did. Still, it didn't change how I felt about what he did to me.

"Teyanna trying to break us up is part of the problem. She had a plan way before she came to you with her fake ass cancer. I'm angry that you lied and said she was your cousin instead of being honest with me. You could have come to me and told me the situation, and we could have found a solution to the problem. Instead, you lied to me and continued to have this bitch in my home. With all of that, that's not the worst part. You acted like my mother and treated me like I was crazy. That was the worst thing you could do to me. Grizz, you didn't believe in me." My voice broke as I wiped away a tear. I thought I was done crying, but this shit hurt me more than he knew.

I spent years with my mother treating me and my mental disease like it was a joke and not believing me. She told me one time she thought I did all of this to get out of going to school. To this day, she still treated me like that and called me names like crazy, crazy bitch, or loco. Knowing your mother did that shit was hurtful enough, but for the man who I felt saved me and showed me that someone is capable of loving someone like me, the shit hurt.

Grizz stood up and came and sat down beside me. I leaned forward and poured the rest of the bottle of wine into my glass. Gently, Grizz took the bottle from my hand and looked at me in the eyes. He set the bottle down and took his hand and held my face in his hands. My heart still went crazy for him. As much as I hated him, I still loved the hell out of this man.

"Dae, you know I never meant to do that shit to you. I love you with all your flaws and all. You mean the world to me, and if I could take back the shit I did to you, I would." Tears fell down his eyes as he looked at me. "I love you, baby. Losing you and then our baby broke me the fuck up. I'm not blaming Teyanna 'cause this shit was all me. I was blinded, and I allowed myself to fall for the shit she was doing. I didn't mean to hurt you, baby. You know I would never do anything to intentionally hurt you. That's why I forced you to the hospital when I did notice you weren't acting like yourself."

"You hurt me, Grizz. Like, I've never felt so hurt in my life. And I didn't think it would come from the man I loved more than anything."

Grizz grabbed my face and kissed me on the lips and then pulled his head back and looked into my eyes. "I want this... I want us. Sundae, I'm not going to stop fighting until I have you back. I know this shit gonna take some time and you need time to think, but I want you." He slipped a key into my hand.

I looked at him confused. "What is this to?"

"To my heart," he said, and I started laughing as I wiped away my tears.

"Why are you being so corny? What is this to?" I continued to laugh. It was something that was needed to lighten the mood.

"I wanted to see you smile again." He wiped the tears from my eyes. "It's the key to our new condo. The other house has too many bad memories for us, and I want to start fresh and new. Manic had me thinking of buying real estate, so I had bought this condo and was going to rent it out, but it can be the start of something new between the both of us."

"I reall—"

"I don't need an answer today, tomorrow, or even next month. I just need you to hold onto the key and use it when you're ready. I'll be there... forever." He kissed me on the lips and got up from the couch.

"Okay," I whispered and held the key in my hands.

"I love you, Sundae."

"I know," I replied and walked over to the door near him. He pulled me into one of his bear hugs that I loved so much. Afterward, he opened the door and looked at me once more before he walked down the hall.

I closed the door behind me and leaned on it after it was already closed. Only time would tell if I would ever use this key. Right now, I needed to work on myself and work through the hurt that I felt. Grizz was who I wanted to be with, even though he hurt me. However, just because I *wanted* to be with him didn't mean I was *supposed* to be with him.

T hree Months Later....

"DAMN, TWEET. CAN I GET SOME PEPPER FOR MY EGGS!" I hollered from the bed. Tweeti came into our bedroom with the pepper and the ketchup.

"Nigga, I was feeding your son." She huffed and slammed the pepper and ketchup on the bedside table before walking out the room. "Oh, and the next time we bet on something, I'm not fucking fixing your breakfast," she turned around and told me.

Nobody told her ass to bet me on my mama. When I first was discharged from the hospital, everyone came over to my crib every day. Especially my mother. She would bring her chef to fix food and spend all day here with us. I told Tweeti that the shit would slow up the longer I was home. Tweeti wanted to place a bet that my mother would still be over-bearing and would continue to come over every day like she'd been doing. That shit died, and my mother called, but she hadn't been over here in a solid month. It was either she make me breakfast in bed or she fuck the shit out of me. Since we'd been fucking like rabbits since I got home, I opted for the breakfast since her ass never made me none.

A nigga really tried to kill my ass. When Uzi told me who the fuck tried to kill me, I was shocked. A fucking pig tried to kill me because of his brother snaking my brother. How the fuck did that shit work? His brother was playing the game wrong and got caught up in his shit. Why the fuck should I pay with my life because he got popped for being grimy? And then his moms, well, shit, that was her own fault. The world needed less crackheads anyway. I scooped some grits on my spoon and laid back and closed my eyes as I savored the taste. I'd been home three months, and the shit felt good. It felt nice to finally be home around my family and lying next to my wife every night.

If it was one thing I could change, it would be Tweeti being so damn overprotective. She didn't want me out in the streets and wanted me home with her and Taz all day. We left to go shopping, but other than that, we were in the crib all day. As much as I loved my wife and son, I just wanted to chill and go see what the fuck was going on in the streets. Just because I almost lost my life didn't mean that I was going to give it up. My phone buzzed next to me, and I looked at Zuri's name coming across my screen. I slid my greasy finger across my screen and hit the speaker button.

"Yo, what's good?"

"I need to head out of town this week. You know I'm opening the boutique with my best friend in Miami, right?"

"Yeah, you told me something about it."

"Well, I need to go down there to go over inventory and stuff," she explained on the phone. "Did you want the nanny to stay with the girls, or did you want me to bring them over your house?"

Tweeti and Zuri finally sat down and talked, then the kids met each other. Blending my family was important to me. I wanted my wife and baby mother to get along, not just for the kids, but for each other. If I would have died, they would have had to stick together for my kids. Tweeti was fine knowing that what me and Zuri had was years ago. Zuri just wanted to know that Tweeti wouldn't treat them any different because they weren't her kids. Once Tweeti told her that if they got out of line, she wouldn't hesitate to put them back in line like she would do to Taz. They got their mutual under-standing, shit had been smooth sailing.

The girls came over three times a week after school. Zuri had her hands in all types of businesses and was just trying to secure the bag for the girls. How could I be mad at that or stand in the way of that? I knew what she was doing was for our daughters, and I had to respect that. She could easily have her hands out, but she didn't. Instead, she realized that she got my respect from her working hard and earning the money like I did mine, though I still covered half the twin's bills and she covered the other half. We both had to learn that we were a team and that the twins depended on both of us. We couldn't continue to act in our feelings, because that would end up hurting the girls more.

"You can bring them over here. The nanny can come too, if she wants."

"Yeah, okay, so Tweeti could be hollering. She already told me she don't like the nanny." Zuri laughed. "But fine, I'll bring the girls over after school. I need to bring anything?"

"Zuri, they have a whole bedroom with shit. Just bring their book bag and that's it," I told her.

"Okay. We'll see you later." I ended the call and got back

to eating my food. Taz entered the room first, and Tweeti followed behind him.

"Who was that?" she asked as she looked into the top drawer where she kept Taz's pajamas. Because his room was upstairs and ours was downstairs, she kept small shit down here, so she didn't have to run up and down the stairs to get him stuff.

"Zuri. She has to go to Miami for the store. She wanted to know if she should bring the girls here or leave them with the nanny."

"Well, she should bring them here. While she's gone, they can be with us. I don't see why y'all pay that nanny when I'm here."

"Because you'll be back in school soon. You took off for a bit, but you'll be going back soon, and we'll need to hire one for Taz too."

"No the hell we not. My mama does a good job taking care of him, especially now that we got her that new car."

Evelyn did a good ass job when it came to making sure that Taz was taken care of. She took him to all his little baby music classes and spent so much time with him while I was healing up. Taz loved the hell out of his grandmother too. He called her *his* Mimi. I didn't mind Evelyn living with us because we had more than enough room. Not to mention, the twins loved her too. Having family and support around us meant a lot because recovery had been hard as fuck on us. When I first came home, mentally, I felt great. However, my body didn't match my mental. What I thought I could do, I couldn't. It was frustrating as fuck trying to get back to being me. Tweeti had to give me sponge baths and shit. I wasn't a hundred percent, but I felt back to normal. I could transfer myself to and from shit like before. The only thing that I hated was that I couldn't stand on my walker anymore. The pain was unbearable, and I couldn't get my legs to move again. The shit hurt my pride more than anything else.

My physical therapist came by and told me that with work, we could get me back up and walking again. Still, I didn't know if I was up to that challenge yet. Before, my motivation was Taz. I wanted to be able to walk for my son. Now, all I cared about was being alive for my kids. My girls and son knew that I couldn't walk, and they loved me the same. Maybe one day I'd be ready to get back into therapy and shit, but right now, my mental wasn't on that shit, and Tweeti agreed with me. At first, she was on my ass to continue with therapy, but now she saw that I wasn't in the right head space to do the shit. I wasn't saying I wouldn't ever get up and try to walk again, but I was enjoying being able to fucking breathe and enjoy my family right now.

"You right," I finally replied to her. "When you going to talk to your sister?" I brought up. Remi and Tweeti were the most stubborn sisters I had ever met.

The two of them hadn't spoken in months, and neither of them were in a rush to sit down and talk. Remi and Uzi weren't walking down the aisle anymore. The wedding was called off, and Remi was living in my pop's condo he had when he and my mother were separated. This baby shit was way out of hand. The shit that had me laughing at the whole thing was the fact that she and Uzi were still fucking around. They weren't together or getting married, but he still would slide over to the condo and bust her cheeks, and then they wouldn't speak to each other. I thought once Tweeti found out that her sister moved out of his brownstone that she would rush to be by her side. Nah. She continued on like she hadn't heard me tell her the damn news myself.

"When I get around to it," she snapped. "Why you so worried in the first place?" She climbed in the bed and sat Indian style.

"That's your sister, babe. You two are close as fuck, and neither of you have said a word to each other in months. You don't see where that shit is crazy?"

"Nope."

"Quit playing."

She sighed and grabbed Taz who was trying to head into our bathroom. "I miss my sister, I do. These past few months, I didn't see her reaching out to me. She's reached out to Sundae to hang out and shit, but has she called me?"

"You've reached out to Sundae and Paisley to hang out, and have you reached out to her?" She flipped me the middle finger.

"Why the hell are you on her side?"

"Fuck!" Taz yelled out.

"Oooohhh, Mimi!" Tweeti yelled, and Taz covered her mouth with his lips.

"Shhh, Mama, shhh! Mimi pow pow," he told her, and I died laughing.

"If you know it's wrong, stop cussing, or I'm telling," she told him, and he gave her that same smirk he inherited from me.

"Ugh, he looks just like you when he's up to no good."

"My pride and joy." I smirked. "I'm not on her side; I'm on the side of what's right. Neither of you are right. You think she's selfish, well, you are too. Maybe not as selfish as she is, but that's something you both share. You think she cares about herself, but so do you. Y'all both have flaws, and neither of you are in the position to judge the other. Make that shit right. You saw what happened to me."

"Whatever." She waved me off. "I'll think about it."

Tweeti saw firsthand how you may lose the chance to tell someone how much they meant to you. With what happened to me, she almost lost that chance. We were beefing and meeting with divorce lawyers all because of a bitch that had a plan to extort money out of my ass. Dakota and her son were long gone. The condo had been cleaned out and sold. Tweeti told me what happened between the both of them, and I was glad I didn't have to deal with her ass. I hadn't heard from her since, and I didn't think I would ever hear from her. It was fine with me because I'd rather put the last few months of our life behind us and move the hell on.

"You ready to try for another baby?" I winked at her.

She smiled at me and looked away. "I've been thinking about it. Enough time has passed since I miscarried, and I want a little girl."

"Nah, I want a little boy. Too many damn girls in this crib, and me and my son need an alliance."

"What the hell you mean?"

"You and the girls tag team my son when I'm not here."

"It's not my fault they know how to get their little brother right. He be clowning when they here." She laughed. "Right, Tazzy?"

He smiled a silly grin and played with her chain. The one thing about having Evelyn here was that she was able to wean my son off breast milk. Tweeti wasn't breastfeeding, pumping, or none of that shit anymore. Not to mention, our son didn't crowd our room anymore. Evelyn had him sleeping through the night in his own damn bed. Having my wife to myself felt good, but the need for another baby was there. When Tweeti miscarried, it broke the both of us. Even though we were going through a tough time when she found out that she was pregnant, it was still something exciting to look forward to.

"I'm ready to put another seed in you, Tweeti McKnight."

"Well, I'm ready when you are, Mr. McKnight." She blushed and got off the bed. "Let me go make sure the twin's room is together before they get here. And I need to run to the store so I can have their afterschool snack ready."

"I appreciate you, baby." She came over to my side of the

bed and bent down to kiss me on the lips. "You know I love you, right?"

"And you know I love you, right?"

"For sure," I replied.

"I'll be back in a little while. Get out of bed, shower, and change before they come. Your bet is over... I need you to empty that dishwasher."

"Damn, I thought this bet was for breakfast, lunch, and dinner?"

"Don't play yourself. Or you won't get dessert later." She slapped that fat ass of hers and looked back at me.

"I gotta go meet with my pops. He wants to talk to me and Uzi about something."

"Make sure you have Grizz drive you."

"Bet." I got out the bed so I could start my day and then end it by hopefully putting a baby in Tweeti tonight.

MY POPS HAD US MEET HIM AT THIS CONDOMINIUM THAT HE had just bought downtown Brooklyn. It was right in the heart of Brooklyn, and with them building condos everywhere, it was the perfect time for the McKnight family to own a building. He made sure to make sixteen of the units for low income families. Since we all came from the hood, my father loved to find a way to give back to families that weren't as fortunate as we were. I respected my pops for doing that because not a lot of businessmen gave a fuck about the people with low income. All they cared about was securing funds and not enough about the people they were hurting in order to secure those funds.

We were sitting downstairs in the new manager's office, waiting for my pops. He walked in with his assistant. She greeted us then went on about her business with her little agenda in her hand. He hugged us both and then sat behind the desk.

"Traffic is crazy," he said and took his suit jacket off. "How's the wives and the grandkids?" He broke the ice with asking about our women and his grandkids. My father loved having grandchildren. When he wasn't away on business, he would have them over his house. Taz was infatuated with his grandfather.

"I'm single, Pops. And, Paris is good. She's still applying to colleges and shit. The damn application process got me going crazy.'"

"You know we can just pay to get her into any college that she wants to attend, right?"

"Yeah, but I'm trying to let her be normal. It's looking like she want to stay in the city or go to Atlanta."

"Damn, niecey trying to get away from us," I joked.

"She not staying in no damn dorms either," my father added. "A condo in Buckhead would be good for her."

"Pops, let me handle this. I'm her father, remember." Uzi laughed.

"And you?" He turned his attention to me.

"We're good. Tweet and me thinking about trying for another baby. The twins and Taz are good... We really good."

"I'm glad. You and Tweet should try for another one. I could use some more grandchildren." He laughed.

"Yeah... What's with this meeting?" I cut the small talk. My father was busy, and very rarely did he call a meeting with us. If he wanted to catch up, he would do that by calling or stopping by.

"I'm telling the both of you because I know that you both can handle it better than your sister. I'm leaving your mother... again."

"I saw it coming," I said.

I wished I could say I was surprised by what he said, but the truth was that I wasn't. I knew he and my mother weren't going to last because she didn't change. My mother was still the woman who cared too much about everyone's opinion and catered to my father. While most men wanted a woman like that, my father wanted a woman that was going to tell him no, and live life at her own terms, not his. It was part of the reason he went for younger women. They didn't give a damn about catering to their men. All they knew was to fuck him so good that he'd come back begging for more, and apparently, that's what Pops liked.

"You couldn't fill me in on it?" Uzi turned to me.

"Nah, I didn't know for sure, but I was thinking that it wasn't going to work this time." Hell, I had my own shit to worry about. I couldn't sit and worry about if my parents were going to break up again.

"What makes this shit crazy is that big ass estate that you both had built. Why did you do all that shit if you didn't want to be with her?" I asked.

"Your mother is familiar to me. She's what I'm used to, and after being together all those years then divorcing, I was missing her. I saw how young, fun, and different she was being while dating, and I wanted that Emory. At first, that's the Emory I got. The one that would suc—"

"Give me a second to rip my fucking ears off and put them on the table!" I yelled and covered my ears. "This is my mama you're talking about."

"I'm sorry." He laughed and fixed his tie. "All I'm saying is that she was fun. Emory wasn't worried about country clubs and impressing people; it was about me and her. Now, she's joined the country club in our new neighborhood, and she's all about impressing everyone there. I'm sick of the shit. I want a woman that's gonna slap the shit out of me when I'm talking down to her and tell me to check myself; not a woman that will tell me she'll do better. Emory used to be that chick, and now she's this Stepford wife I don't even want to lay beside every night. I'm not happy. I need to be happy."

"Pops, everyone deserves to be happy. I'm just saying, your happiness comes with a price, and that price is my mama's heart. She can't go through this shit again." Uzi laid out the facts. My mother was going to be heartbroken again, and this time, who knew what the fuck she would do. The same nigga she allowed back in her life was stabbing her in the heart again. That shit was enough to have someone ready to jump off a fucking roof.

"I met someone. I'm in love, and for the first time, I see us being something. She doesn't want to be my side chick forever, and I have to make an honest woman out of her."

"Yo, I feel like I'm in the fucking Twilight Zone or something. What the hell do you mean you need to make an honest woman out of her? She's a fucking side chick... All she's supposed to do is take dick, money, and be quiet." Clearly, my pops didn't know how to fucking have a side chick.

"Look, your mother isn't a fucking angel either. Ask her about her damn fascination with the male strippers in Jersey. Came back to me that she fucked one of them too, and we were together."

"Shit, mama a player." I laughed.

"Y'all need to end the shit. At the end of the day, the shit is unhealthy. You need to tell her it's over and let it be over. I got my own shit I'm dealing with!" Uzi barked and slammed his hands on the table.

"You and Remi?" I looked over at him.

"Yeah. I didn't think we would be in this place. After we fuck, I put my jeans on and bounce. Like, shorty is pissed that I called off the wedding and engagement."

"You calling it off was for a very good reason. She doesn't want children, and you do. You can't get married having differences like that, because in the end, you'll end up hating her," my father schooled him.

"In the end, you both need to make it work for each other. If being together isn't the plan, then end it and be friends," I added.

"Yeah, I hear y'all." He sighed.

We sat and chilled with my father for a little while before I got ready to head home. My pops needed to talk to my mother and make sure this was what he wanted to do. He couldn't have her out here thinking their shit was perfect when it wasn't. My father wasn't happy, and I couldn't blame him. Yet, he needed to handle his responsibility like a man before he could ride off into the sunset with his side chick that wanted to be an honest woman.

❧ 14 ❧

PAISLEY

Seven months. I made it to seven months pregnant, and baby girl was getting bigger by the day. I was so happy that my pregnancy was progressing and there hadn't been any issues as of yet. I was still supposed to take it easy, but it was hard to do with a two-year-old. Sayana was so busy and wanted to get into everything there was. I had to finally break down and have someone come and baby proof the apartment. In the end, it would be good for Sayana and for the new baby when she came. Ms. Vee came and visited when she could, and tried to be a part of Sayana's life, but with her mother's health declining, she was always busy with her, and I understood. The one smart thing about Syria was that she had life insurance. The policy was for a hundred thousand dollars. Ms. Vee was the beneficiary and made sure she opened an account for Sayana, and when she was older, she would be able to touch the money. In the meantime, only me and Ms. Vee had access to the money.

At first, it was hard to adjust to raising Sayana again. I had gotten used to doing whatever I wanted and not having to care for a child. Then, I had to deal with mourning over

Rome. Manic was there through everything and didn't get mad when I woke up screaming and crying during the night. He understood that me and Rome had history, even if it wasn't good history, it was still history, and it was emotional for me. Then I cried for Syria because she would never get to see her baby girl grow up. Sayana would never see her mother because she died while Sayana was too young. All of that stuff took a while to get over. Sayana cried the first week or so she moved into the apartment with me. Now, things were going well and we were both adjusting to things. I had gone and got her a mini toddler's bed that was right beside mine, and then the crib was on the other side of the bed for when Aubree came.

Nisha was about to hit nine months and was still doing the most. Manic was trying so hard to be in two places at once, but the truth was, he couldn't. With Nisha being further along than me, he had to be there for her the most right now. This was tiring him out because when he came over, he would literally be asleep within seconds. I was trying so hard to be the good girlfriend that understood, but Nisha was making it hard for me. Like this baby shower we had to attend today. She made sure to send me an invitation to their gender reveal and baby shower. Manic told me that I didn't have to go, but why wouldn't I go? With me not going, I was allowing her to act like she and my man were this perfect couple about to welcome a baby. Hell no. I wasn't about to give her that, so I was going to attend, smile, and make sure everyone knew that she and Manic were not together.

"Damn, you still not dressed. Where's lil' mama's clothes?" Sayana ran over to him, and he picked her up.

Manic had been amazing when it came to Sayana. She had gotten so used to him and loved messing with his colorful hair. She loved being around him, and he loved being around her too. He told me that it got him prepared for when our little girl came. Nisha still hadn't told him what she was having. She wanted to wait until the baby shower so she could have the reveal and shower the same day. If you asked me, I thought the idea was stupid as hell. Here she was doing the most instead of just having a damn shower and finding out the sex of her baby like everyone else did.

"I just bathed her, and now I'm about to dress her. She heard your voice and jumped down from the bed," I answered and went to grab her little shoes off the dresser.

"Baby, you need more room. You got the crib over there and then the toddler bed over there. You know there's only gonna be more shit when Aubree comes, right?"

It was true. The bedroom that was meant for just me was full to capacity. I had Sayana's stuff all over the place, and then I had Aubree's stuff in the corner near her crib. Since Sundae was still staying here, I had to make it work with the space I had. Hell, I wasn't complaining. Long as me and my girls had a roof over our head, I didn't care. Keeping them close to me was all I cared about right now. Sayana had gotten used to climbing in the bed with me during the night. Just imagine when Aubree was here, and we all laid in the bed together. It warmed my heart just thinking of it.

"It's fine, babe. I'm not complaining."

"Hell, I am. It feels like we're in a damn studio apartment. Sundae is barely even here like that," he pointed out.

Sundae had been traveling the world. What started out as a eat, pray, and love retreat in Bali, ended with her deciding to travel all around the world. This girl spent time in Dubai, Africa, Jamaica—she went everywhere. She sat me down and told me how she felt like she was about to spiral downhill again and needed something new and fresh. She showed me this retreat in Bali and told me that it was for two weeks, and she just needed to get away before she resorted back to her old ways. Being that she had suffered from a mental breakdown the week before, I knew she needed this more than the air to breathe. Me and Tweeti drove her to the airport and cried the whole way there. We knew she needed this, but it didn't make it less hard to ship our friend off. What some thought was minor, she and Grizz went through something that shook her entire core. It changed how she viewed someone she loved with every fiber of her being. That wasn't something she could just shake away and move past. It was going to take a lot of soul searching for her to decide if she really wanted to move on from she and Grizz's relationship or if she wanted to work on fixing what they had.

"She comes back next week. I'm not going to just move her out her room because she's traveling the world."

"Well, shit. You need to move in with me because I got more room. I don't want my baby coming into the world being claustrophobic."

I laughed and tossed the shoe at him. "Shut up. We're blessed to just have a roof over our head. And move in? You sure we're ready for that?"

"Why you keep getting scared when I bring up moving in together? We're about to have a whole baby, and you're scared to live with me." It was true.

It was like I froze up whenever he brought up us moving in together. It wasn't that I was scared; okay, maybe I was scared. When we needed our space, we lived apart and could have that. If we decided to move in together, we wouldn't be able to escape each other. I just didn't want us to end up fighting and break up before Aubree could be born.

"I have baggage now. It's not just me anymore. I have Sayana now."

"And you acting like I don't know that. Jelly bean is a part of you, and she comes wherever you go. Why you keep acting like I'm gonna treat her different because of the hate I hold for her pops? Jelly bean didn't have no part of that, so I would never hold that on her."

"I know... I just don't want you to feel like I'm pushing her on you... you know?"

"Paisley, you're not pushing her on me. I see her every day. Did you not think we would build a bond? Far as I'm concerned, she's going to be my daughter's big sister. It ain't the most normal setup, but that's life. Hell, I'm not the most normal nigga."

"You're right," I agreed.

This wasn't the most practical setup, but this was my life, and I had to deal with it. Sayana needed a home, and foster care wasn't an option. Especially with me having a place to lay my head, I was going to give her one too. Both her parents were shit, but they deserved to have their daughter raised and treated like the princess that she was.

"Shit, I know." He slid the dress over Sayana's head and put her on the floor. "You gonna think about it, or we going to move in together?" He moved toward me and rubbed my stomach. At seven months, my stomach had popped literally overnight.

At first, Manic was accusing me of hiding his baby from him because my belly was small. Once I got over that five-month hump, my stomach was growing, and I was relieved. The last thing I wanted was for my baby to be born small or with complications. Even though my stomach getting bigger didn't secure that, it was something I told myself to stop from worrying so much.

"I'm sorry about today," he apologized.

"You don't need to apologize. I'm going to support you and only you." I kissed him on the lips. "Okay?"

"Ight. This shit just feels weird as fuck. We not inviting her to our baby shower though."

"We're not having a baby shower though. A cute little brunch is fine."

"You inviting your mom?"

I shrugged. Manic met my mother briefly last month. She was in the hospital for her gallbladder, and I went up to visit her. He came with me and met her. Her boyfriend at the time came in the room, and she acted as if she didn't want us there anymore. I could tell from the bruise on her arm that he was beating her ass. I prayed that she found someone who loved her hard enough where she saw that this abuse wasn't the only answer. My mother was a beautiful, smart, and kind woman, and she deserved for a man to love her for the good woman she was. Like I had to learn, I prayed she learned before the next time I saw her was in a grave.

"We'll see."

"I'm not going to push it. If you want to tell her, you can tell her. If not, then she doesn't need to be there."

"Thank you."

"You're welcome. Let's get ready to go because the limo is waiting."

"Limo?"

"Nah, I'm fucking with you." He laughed.

I put my heels on, and we headed out the door. We headed to the parking garage and got in what Manic called his dad car. He had a Tahoe. I didn't know why the fuck he needed such a large truck when he was only having two babies, but I didn't question him. Even with Sayana, he still didn't need this much space. If he thought more babies were coming out of me after Aubree, he was crazy as hell.

"Can you help me climb up in here?" I asked after he finished fastening Sayana's car seat. He helped me into the front seat, and I got settled.

"I'm nervous as fuck," he admitted when he got into the car.

"Why?"

"I never drove this big shit before."

"Are you serious? Why the hell you bought it in the first place?"

"I'm not driving no damn minivan. This was the next best thing." He explained his crazy ass logic.

"You have two kids. Not six or fifteen, so your car you had would have been fine. Take this big ass truck back."

"Nah, I need my dilf car," he disagreed with me.

"I'm not arguing with you. All I know is we better end up there safe, and remember your daughter is riding shotgun." I pointed to my stomach.

"Well shit, Paisley. No pressure, huh?"

"Humph." I smacked my lips and leaned back in the chair.

I watched as he whipped this big car out the spot with one hand and headed out the parking garage. He did damn good for someone who was nervous about driving this big ass truck. We drove all the way to this venue Nisha had picked in Long Island. It was a golf club where she had rented out their hall. It was a nice place, but it was too extra for just a baby shower. The thing that pissed me off was that she went all out because Manic's money paid for it. When Manic and I first started messing around, he told me about Nisha and told me how she was independent and didn't take shit from nobody.

The more I saw her, she wasn't any of those things that he described. She wasn't independent, because Manic had somehow got roped into paying her bills and shit. She loved to whine and say it was because her other baby daddy was locked up. The bitch was just used to being cash flowed by niggas, and now she had to use Manic. Me? I still worked my assistant job and had gotten a raise. All my money was stacked in my account, and I still paid Manic every month on payday. He hated it, but I loved having my independence. I didn't have to depend on him for anything. When I slid my card to pay for something without having to use his money, it felt so freeing. I was able to shop for our baby girl and didn't have to ask him for money. Of course when we went shopping for Aubree together, he paid for her stuff. Being able to provide for Sayana without having to ask anyone for money was a feeling I wasn't used to. When I worked at the dental office, I brought home a check and handed it over to Rome. He gave me the money I needed for the week, and that was that. Thinking back, I was a damn fool to work hard all week and hand my money over to a nigga that didn't bother to give me a ride to work in the morning. Man, I was glad that I wasn't in that mental place anymore.

"This place looks expensive," I commented as we walked inside the building. Manic held Sayana and held the gray Birkin purse he bought me as push present. I didn't want to know how much this bag cost because I would be tempted to return the bag

"It was. Eight bands to secure this spot. She wouldn't have it anywhere else," he mumbled and kissed me on the lips. "I love you, baby."

"I love you too, babe," I replied, and when we broke our kiss, I saw Nisha standing there with this glitter dress on, covering her big basketball shaped stomach. Her makeup was too dramatic, and she had bundles that were spiral-curled down to her ass.

"About time you showed up. We need to go take some pictures... You mind if I take him?" Nisha asked me snottily.

I laughed and took Sayana from him. "Go ahead."

"Jelly bean, walk," Manic told Sayana, and she motioned for me to put her down. He hated when I held her because he didn't want anything to happening to me and the baby.

"I'm here... Why the fuck is this so far?" My baby Tweeti came in at the right time. I needed back up because I knew

Nisha would have Manic the entire event. When I called, she told me to tell her the place and she would be there.

"Ask disco ball Barbie." I rolled my eyes.

Taz had a little crush on Sayana, and they played together all the time. When Sayana saw him, she ran over to hug him and kiss him on the cheek. "Oh, she look loud." Tweeti used her hand as a fan. "I put makeup and shit on for this?"

"She just pulled him away." I informed her on what had just happened.

"You good, 'cause I would have been right in the pictures too. Fuck outta here." She rolled her eyes.

We made our way to the main room where everything was set up. The room was decorated in mint green, yellow, and white. Since she didn't know what she was having, there was no set color. We found the table she had assigned us and sat down. The kids went to play in the little bubble pit that she had set up for kids that attended.

"Why she trying so hard?" Tweeti asked as she accepted the drink from the waiter. "What the hell she need all this for?"

"'Cause she has his money to spend being extra. She didn't need to do any of this." I sighed.

"And when are we going to plan yours? 'Cause you know we gotta go ten times harder and invite her ass."

"Nope, I'm doing a brunch. I don't want anything big, honestly."

"I understand, babe. The only reason I disagree is because this pregnancy has been hard on you and your body. You deserve to celebrate Aubree coming into this world."

"Can I be honest?"

"You better."

"I keep waiting for something bad to happen. This pregnancy has been hard but smooth in the same sentence. I haven't had to be admitted to the hospital or anything, so consider that good. I'm just worried the complications will come when it's time for her to be born."

"Oh, you Manic's baby mama." Two girls walked over with multicolored hair. I assumed that they must have been Nisha's friends.

"Nah, she's his girl... Why, who the fuck asking?" Tweeti answered before I could. I guess they must have saw that she was with it and decided to switch their approach.

"Oh, we just wanted to make sure you were okay. Let us know if you need anything," the one with the green hair spoke.

"Oh, ight..." Tweeti rolled her eyes. "Y'all need anything, because you still standing here?" Tweeti asked them, and I laughed. They walked away and went back over to their table.

"I swear I can't take you no damn where."

"Shit, they came over here like they were pressing somebody. I haven't had no dick and I'm on my period. Go ahead and try it. I'll beat some ass today."

"Chill out, Mike Tyson." I giggled.

Music played, and the double doors opened, and Nisha and Manic walked into the baby shower. Everyone stood up and clapped in excitement when they entered. Me and Tweeti remained seated and rolled our eyes.

"He doesn't even look happy," Tweeti pointed out. Manic looked like he wanted to be any place but here with Nisha at their baby shower. Meanwhile, she was all smiles and waves like this was the best day of her life.

The DJ handed each of them a mic, and she laughed before she spoke. "Hey, everyone. Thank you for coming to me and Mitchell's baby shower. Half of you guys probably knew we would end up here since we all grew up together." She giggled.

"That boy was crazy about you!" one lady yelled out from

the table across from us. Me and Tweeti both looked at that lady like she had lost her mind.

"And he still is. That's how this little baby ended up here." She giggled. "Anyway, we'll get to the part we're all excited about." A waiter rolled this lavish cake with pink and blue dots all over the cake. "You wanna cut, boo?"

The little shit she kept doing was pissing me off, and I could tell it was pissing him off too. He was trying hard not to embarrass her in front of all their friends. "Yeah," he replied.

I stood so I could see. He put his mic down and cut the cake. He pulled the piece out and set it on the plate. Nisha started screaming, yelling, and being extra with her friends. "It's a girl! It's a girl!" she screamed out.

"Yass, she's having Manic's first daughter!" her little friend got on the mic and yelled. Nisha took the mic from her and put it to her mouth.

"Oh my God! I didn't think I was going to have his first daughter. I'm so excited for Aubree to be here."

"Wait, hold the fuck up? Did she just say Aubree?" Tweeti hollered. My heart was beating so fast that I had to sit down to keep from passing out. I was pretty sure Manic had mentioned our daughter's name, and I wasn't mad. However, for her to steal my daughter's name pissed me the fuck off. I couldn't change her name; this was the name we picked since we found out that she was going to be a girl.

"Mitchell, you got something to say about your new baby girl coming."

He took his mic and looked out to the crowd. "Yeah, I do." He cleared his throat. "Paisley, where you at?"

"Right here!" Tweeti yanked me to my feet.

"Baby, since the day I met you, I knew that you were my one. You fuck a bunch of bitches, but you only get one love. You were that one for me, and I knew I would spend the rest of my life trying to be the perfect man, because shit, if I wanna be honest, I still don't believe I deserve you." He walked closer to me. "I tell you damn near every day that you're my dream girl, and now that you're having my baby, I want to make this official." He got down on his knee and pulled a box out of his back pocket. "Will you marry me, Paisley?"

I held my hands over my mouth and looked down at him as tears fell from my face. Sayana ran over and hugged my leg and was looking up in my face trying to figure out what was wrong with me. The ring was a pear-shaped halo five carat ring in white gold. It was so beautiful I stood there admiring the ring.

"Damn, you gonna say something?" Tweeti brought me back to reality.

"Yes." I smiled and nodded my head. I pulled him up, and he slid the ring on my finger, then kissed me so deep that my knees were weak. I loved when he had his hair pulled up in a bun. The way he was staring at me told me everything I needed to know. I was his one.

"Really, Mitchell! You wait to do this shit at my baby shower?" Nisha was nearly in tears as she watched everything go down from the front.

"Fuck outta here... You thought you was about to make my fiancée look stupid. Even after you went and stole the name I told you she was naming our daughter, she still sat there and didn't fuck up your baby shower." He spoke to her through the mic, and Tweeti was laughing so hard. "Baby, I'm sorry for even putting you in a situation like this. I respect you way too much for you to sit here while a bunch of bitches try to disrespect you when you've been nothing but respectful. Nisha, you crossed the line." He picked up Sayana, held my hand, and we left out the doors. Tweeti was right behind us, laughing and snickering. Nisha's face was on the floor as she watched her baby daddy leave their baby shower with me, his fiancée.

"Congratulations, guys. I'm so happy for you both." Tweeti smiled and hugged both of us. "And Manic, it takes a real man to step up and stand up for his woman. Those bitches definitely were trying to make her look stupid, and you did what was right."

"Appreciate it. I just want to do right by my dream girl." He pulled me close and kissed me on the lips.

"Awe, you got me ready to head home and be kind to my husband," she joked.

"Thank you, baby. You didn't have to do that. I was there for you, not for Nisha and all her foolishness."

"Yeah, and that's why I did it. I've been carrying this ring for a month. I wanted to do it somewhere unexpected. A few times I almost did it at the grocery store but decided against it. This right here couldn't have been more perfect."

Nisha stormed out the doors and headed straight to Manic. "You're so fucked up. I've been there with you since kids, and you do me like this." She sobbed.

"History don't have shit to do with what's going on. You knew my daughter with Paisley was going to be named Aubree, and you decided to be petty and do that shit in front of everyone. You wanted to fucking make a fool out of her, and now you look like the fucking fool. Why you trying to hurt someone that has never hurt you?"

"She has. Look, she's having a baby and with you. I told you I loved you, and you didn't bat an eyelash or even try and make it work. Instead, you decided to be with this homeless bitch."

"I told you already about disrespecting her."

"You disrespected her when you brought her to our baby shower."

"And I know that. Like a real man, I was able to right my wrongs and realize that I fucked up."

"Real man?" She spit at his feet. "You're a kid trying to be a man."

"Yeah, but you wanted this little kid dick though, right?" He grabbed his dick through his slacks. "If I tossed this dick to you tomorrow you would fucking catch this shit with your mouth. Stop trying to play me. I'm a grown ass man and handle my shit like one. If I wasn't a man, neither of you would have known about the other. I would have hid that shit and wouldn't have said shit. You don't like Paisley, that's fine. However, you will respect her. And name my daughter Aubree, and you'll have a fucking issue with me."

"I'll name her what the fuck I want."

"And see what the fuck will happen. Just because I been cool, don't forget what the fuck I'm capable of." He winked at her and grabbed my hand. "You hungry?"

"Yes." I giggled.

"Let me feed my three babies." He laughed and grabbed Sayana's little hand. Tweeti hugged us and told us she was going to do some shopping and then head home. She congratulated us then went to her car. Today had been too much, but I was so damn happy that I had a good man.

❧ 15 ❧

TWEETI

Enough time had passed, and it was time for me to sit down and speak to my sister. I knew she wasn't going to come to me, so I got the address to where she was staying, and I was going to her. Remi was far too spoiled to come to me and fix what we both knew needed to be fixed. If I had to be honest, I missed my sister, and we let something small get way out of hand. We both were wrong and needed to fix this so we could move on. She was going through something in her life, and I needed to be there for her. Even though she was a damn ghost when it came to being there for me, it didn't mean I had to do the same. You didn't do people how they did you because that karma, baby, was nothing to be messed with. Your blessings would come tenfold when you continued to be you and not trying to be grimy to get back at the person.

I held my purse and knocked on the door and waited for her to answer. The slippers sliding across the floor told me that she was home. Even if she tried to act like she wasn't, I had Paisley call her and act like she wanted to hang out. Remi told her that she was tired and staying in the house to watch movies all day. The door swung open, and she looked at me with a raised brow.

"If you came to argue, save it," she told me and held the door opened for me. "What's up?"

I walked in and looked around the lavish condo that had been her home for the past few months. "I came over here to talk. I'm not arguing with you."

"Good, that makes two of us. How did you find out where I was staying?"

"Your man told me."

"Figures. He don't know how to keep his mouth shut. Oh, and he's not my man anymore... you didn't hear?"

"I've heard."

"Well, the wedding is over. Did you come over here to tell me it's because I'm selfish?" She leaned against the marble counters.

"Rem, I didn't come over here for all of that. I came over to tell you that I miss my sister and want to be her baby sis again. It doesn't matter who is selfish and who isn't. You're still my sister and I love you."

She broke down. "I missed the hell out of you and needed you. Mama tries to help, but she's not you." She sobbed. "I should have been there for you when Jah was going through everything. I beat myself up every day for that."

"I know, baby girl... It's okay, and I'm not angry with you about it either. We got through that, and he's fine." I walked around the counter and hugged her. "I love you, and I'm always going to be here for you."

"Tweet, I'm pregnant," she revealed, and I pulled back from her. Last I remembered, she and Uzi were arguing and broken up because she didn't want to have any kids.

"I'm so confused." I sat down on the island and stared at her.

"He doesn't know yet. I found out last month and have

been keeping quiet about it. I'm scared and don't know if I want to keep it."

"Rem, if you have an abortion and he finds out... you know the both of you will be done for good, right?"

"I know." She ran her hands through her hair. "I'm so fucking scared that I don't want to do anything. I'm scared to work out or do small shit like going to the grocery store."

"Rem... you have to realize that a miscarriage will happen. There's nothing we can do about it. Just continue to pray."

"That's all I've been doing," she told me.

"And apparently, you and Uzi still be fucking... Y'all got all of us thinking you both are done."

She smiled. "It's not the same. We have sex, he leaves, and we don't speak. He's angry, and when he's mad, he shuts people out."

"Was it your idea for you to leave?"

"No." She looked down. "It was his. He told me he was tired of seeing me around the house. That I was just a reminder of another failed relationship."

"Damn."

"Yeah. He was going to put me up in a hotel, but I called Shad, and he told me to come stay here."

"Shad's a good guy. It's that damn Emory that makes me want to pull my hair out."

"Yeah, both she and Wynner aren't talking to me. They're mad that the wedding is off because I'm being foolish—their words."

"Fuck 'em. Wynner over there being stupid in love with a nigga that dogged her out and then wanted to change. Emory over there loving a man that doesn't want to love her back. Of course, they're viewing this as you're being foolish. They have devoted their lives to men that aren't shit."

"You just said Shad is a good guy though."

"Oh, he's a good person, but he ain't worth shit as a man."
I laughed.

"True. I just want us to go back to how we used to be.
Wynner used to hang with us and we would do things
together."

"Wynner has let her mother get way into her head.
Hanging with her is like hanging with a mini Emory. Not to
mention, that girl is too devoted to her kids and husband.
Nothing wrong with that, but she doesn't have a life outside
of those kids and her husband. Wynner is younger than both
of us; that shit is weird."

"And that's what the fuck scares the hell out of me," Remi
blurted.

"What?"

"That I'll have this baby and lose my figure, mental, and
life. I'll then be married and have to devote all my time to my
Uzi, Paris, and the baby. I don't want to lose myself."

"Rem, is this why you didn't want to have any kids?"

"Yes, because I saw it happening to you. You weren't so
focused on Jah, but more on Taz, and, Tweet, you changed. It
was so scary watching."

"I became a mother, Rem. I'm not the same person I was
before Taz was born. In fact, I'm a better person because of
him. I did go through a phase where he was where I focused
all my attention, but I realized that I had a husband that
needed me too."

"And Mama put all that in a smash too."

"That too. You're going to be a good mother, and Uzi is
already a good father. The both of you will find what works
for you both and raise this baby together. You have to get out
your head and stop looking at me or Wynner and thinking
that's going to be you. Every mother is different, and what we
go through or went through may not be what you'll go
through... okay?"

"Thanks, Tweeti."

"Of course... it's why I'm here. Now, when you going to tell him?"

"We got into a fight when he was over here yesterday," she revealed.

"Over?"

"That nigga is dating."

"Wait, what?"

"Uh huh... He's dating some chick, and I don't know who she is. He was honest and told me they went to some concert and out to eat."

"Wait a damn second; he told you he went on a date? You didn't find it out from no one else?"

"Nope. He came over yesterday and told me that he went on a date. He told me that he wasn't young and couldn't sit around praying that this will be fixed. Said he needed to move on until I figured out what I wanted because he didn't just want sex."

"Why the hell is he acting like a bitch with a maternal clock? He can make babies for the rest of his life."

"His reason is because he didn't want to be like Jay- Z being hella old with new kids. I wanted to tell him right then and there, but I was so hurt. He went on a date, and we've only been broken up for three months but are still sleeping together."

"Sex and being together are two different things. He knows you and is comfortable with you, so he comes to get his rocks off and then goes to find a woman that wants the same things as him."

"That hurts more coming out your mouth than it did his."

"Rem, think about it. You've been broken up for three months and nothing has changed. You both are no closer to being back together. Moving on is the next step, and that's what he's doing. It sucks, but he's not wrong for it. And he did better than most men and told you so you wouldn't find out."

"It still hurts."

"Oh, it's gonna hurt. No matter how much it hurts, you need to sit down and talk to him and tell him about the baby. Don't end up trying to hurt him and lose the man you love for good," I advised. Remi was the type that once hurt, she had to hurt you back.

It sucked that Uzi was dating again, but she couldn't be mad because the man was honest with her about everything. I truthfully didn't think that he wanted to date anybody except Remi. This was something to open her eyes and show her that he could and would move on without her. It was a shitty tactic, but I think she was realizing that she loved the hell out of this man and didn't want to lose him.

"I will," she agreed. "I appreciate you coming over and talking to me. Sitting here in my own thoughts were driving me up the wall."

"I could tell. You look like shit and need to go get yourself together before you call him over." I laughed.

"Let me go make a hair appointment." She looked at her nails. "And maybe a nail one too," she added.

"Go ahead and get all done up. That man wants a baby more than anything, so knowing that you're about to have his baby is about to have him excited as hell."

"I know. I'm just nervous to tell him."

"Don't be. And you better tell Emory and Wynner to keep that same ass energy too. You don't need they fake asses in your business."

"I will."

"I'm serious, Rem. Don't let me see on Snapchat you over there getting those expensive ass mani and pedis."

"Alright, but I can't cut them off from being an aunt and grandmother to my baby."

"Why not? Wynner don't even come around Taz, and Emory comes around when Shad wants to take him to their house for the weekend."

"Dang. The way they tell it is like you keep them from coming around."

"So they do be talking shit about me. I knew it, so I'm not surprised."

"Emory may have mentioned it once or twice. Wynner never says anything, but Emory speaks for the both of them."

"Figures."

"All I'm saying is that we have to stick together and make it work. Both of our babies are McKnights, and we have to deal with them for the rest of their lives."

"Speak for yourself. I don't have to deal with toxic people because they are kin to my son. I'm all my son needs, not them."

"We're getting nowhere with this conversation." She laughed.

"Well, you knew you wasn't anyway. After Emory played herself when Jah was in the hospital, that witch can't say more than six words to me."

"I give up." She giggled. "You gotta leave soon?"

"Girl, no. The twins are over, and Jah is over there watching movies and having his time with his kids. I try to have time together as a family and then give him time with his kids."

"Awe, how are you adjusting to the twins and their mom."

"Who, Zuri? Girl, she's cool as hell, and we have a mutual agreement. She drops the twins off, comes inside, chats, and goes about her business. What she and Jah had is over, and I can tell because they act more like damn siblings than baby mama and baby daddy."

"That's nice that everything is coming together for the family. It's important that the kids see a good relationship."

"And that's why I wanted to finally sit down with that woman and talk. I can't be out here acting like a fool over a relationship that happened way before me and him were even together."

"Dang, Taz really changed you," she joshed.

"Shut up." I laughed. "Maybe this baby will change your selfish ass."

"Maybe... then again, I kind of like my selfish ways." She rolled her eyes at me, and we laughed. "Let's watch some movies and order some food in like old times."

I kicked my sneakers off and followed her into the living room. "If you're ordering Chinese food, you already know what I want."

"I'll get the menu," she called from the room.

I plopped on the couch and felt around for the remote. Making up with my sister was something that was well overdue. I was excited that we were able to talk without screaming and yelling. We agreed to disagree, and that was important. We didn't have to agree on everything, but the fact that we could disagree and respect each other's opinion was important to me. Remi got the menu, and I grabbed my cell, and we ordered a shit load of food and found chick flicks on TV. I knew she was going to make me stay the night over, and being away from the kids tonight didn't sound too bad.

I SAT AT THE AIRPORT WAITING FOR SUNDAE TO COME OUT. She was fresh off a flight from Bora Bora. She had been there the longest and was ready to head back to the states. I was excited to have my best friend back. Sending her off on this travel tour she took was the hardest thing I'd ever had to do. I worried about if she decided to go off her meds, where would we find her? Sundae was different, and I had to trust that she would do what was right. This getaway was more for her mental than it was for everything else. She needed to get away and focus on herself. She had been through so much these months that I was sure it would break her, and it did temporarily. When she had her mental breakdown right before she left, I knew this was what she had to do.

Everything was getting to her and hitting her at once, and she flipped. A short trip to the hospital told us what we needed, and she was back right. After that happened, she was more determined than ever to make this trip to Bali for that retreat. With her and Grizz ending, Teyanna trying to fuck up her life, and then losing her baby, I knew she needed to get her life together and focus on something other than her personal life. She needed to get connected with herself and do something for herself.

My girl traveled the world, made friends abroad, and took plenty of pictures. Hell, she had me jealous and ready to jump on a flight to join her a few times. As much as I loved Sundae, I knew I was one of those people she needed a break from too. While dealing with her shit, she was also there for me through my shit. Imagine your entire world falling apart, but you have to be strong for someone else during a crazy time in their life too? Well, that was exactly what it was like for her, and I couldn't understand how she stood strong for so long without breaking?

I clapped my hand when I saw her dragging two suitcases out the airport. Jumping out the car, I ran over to her and jumped all over her. We hugged for what seemed like three hours while kissing each other.

"Oh my God... You've gotten thicker." I spun her around and looked at the ass on her. "Girl, you went and got something done?"

"Hell nah. I don't trust doctors in America, and I damn sure don't trust them over there. I've been working out, eating right, and just getting right," she explained.

"Teach me your ways, because I ate a burger on the way here."

"You so crazy. I missed you, girl." She hugged me again. The toy cops at the airport blew their whistle, which meant we had to move the car. I helped her put her luggage in the back of my car, and we got in.

"Tell me everything. You told me some stuff over the phone, but I want to hear everything." I smiled as I pulled away from the airport.

"I had the most amazing time in my life. Tweet, I prayed so hard that I cried. This trip was more of a spiritual trip for me. I really learned who I am in these three months than all the years I've been alive. Like, I know what my purpose is, and I was able to find myself."

"You know Grizz asked about you every day?" I told her. To do this right, she cut all her communication off with Grizz and shut him out. I wasn't to tell him anything about her, and she didn't want to know anything about him either. It made sense. That was who she was running from, so to get her mind right, she had to cut him out of her life.

"I know. I *had* to do it. If I kept communication with him, I wouldn't have done this. Giving up social media and everything was like a weight was lifted off of me. We're so consumed with social media that we're not living life. I was able to live life and not worry about what anyone's opinion was."

"Your mama asked about you too."

"She was another one."

"She was the main one. I told her you were fine and that's all she needed to know."

"Thank you."

"Of course. I'm just happy you're home."

"Me too." She smiled. "Can we get some food? Oh, I'm vegan too," she decided to add in there.

"Oh hell nah... See, I was with you during the mental shit, but vegan? Sis, you know I love me a good ass steak... Why you doing this?"

"Shut up. I know a good spot that I looked up on the flight here."

"Whatever." I laughed as we headed to go eat Tofu and air. I would eat it all if that meant I got to spend more time with Sundae. I was just happy that she was home.

❧ 16 ❧

SUNDAE

Me and Tweeti spent the day together hanging out and catching up. She filled me in on so much that I felt like I left for six months instead of only three. Everyone was doing good, and I was happy because when I left, it was the opposite. All this positive energy made me feel good about my decision to leave. Taz had run into the end of their coffee table, so Tweeti had to run to meet Jah and Evelyn at the emergency room. I caught an Uber from the bar to home and pulled my bags upstairs. I stood in the hallway and looked at the key. It was the key that I wore around my neck as I traveled all over in those three months. It was the key that Grizz had given me months ago. He told me whenever I was ready to use the key. I was finally ready to put the key into this door and open it.

For three months, I prayed, cried, and laughed over my decision to give him another chance. It was three in the morning, and I didn't know what would be behind that door. He could have moved on with another woman; I didn't know. I didn't want him to be updated on my life, and I didn't want to know anything about him either. After Tweeti left, I spent time in a bar. I didn't drink; I just sat there and thought about my final decision. Did I want to give this man another chance? Was I settling? Or was I trying to make something work that would never work? After my sixth cup of water and a talk with an interesting bartender, I knew that I wanted to make it work with Grizz; not because I was settling or because I was trying to make something work that would never work. I wanted to be with him because he made a terrible mistake, but that was life. We all fucked up, and if someone held our fuck ups over our head, where would we be? In order to move on and be the best woman I could be, I had to let go and let God.

I placed the key in the hole and turned the door. Pulling my bags in behind me, I set them down in the foyer and walked further into this massive penthouse. It was on the top floor and it had huge floor to ceiling windows with a perfect view of the Empire State Building. There was a huge balcony that wrapped around the perimeter of the penthouse. The kitchen was state of the art with a huge quartz countertop. The kitchen and dining area were all in one. I walked down one hall and found three large bedrooms with a bathroom attached to all of them. It was clear he lived here because there was an old bowl of cereal on the kitchen counter. I walked to the other wing of the penthouse and found a double door. It was the only room on this side.

I turned the knob and pushed the door opened. The room was something straight out of a magazine spread. The floor to ceiling windows followed into the bedroom. The light from the Empire State Building gave a beautiful glow into the room. There was a California king size platform bed in the middle of the floor with a sleeping Grizz. I looked into the lavish spa bathroom and smiled at the tub. He knew I loved a deep soaking tub. The bedroom had a seating room, bar, and balcony too. Grizz could sleep through a storm, so I knew that he wouldn't wake up. I stripped down and took a shower in the glass encased shower. It had six showerheads that all sprayed water on me and made me feel like they were wrapping their arms around me. I washed all the traveling funk off me, put lotion on my body, and grabbed one of his big shirts from the closet before slipping into the bed beside him.

I nuzzled my face on his chest and leaned up to kiss him on the lips. After a few kisses, he opened his eyes and realized that he wasn't dreaming anymore. I smiled when his eyes opened wide, and he looked at me confused.

"I had a few drinks, but damn, I know I'm not that fucked up." He mumbled and sat up and turned on the light beside him. "Sundae?"

"Who else would it be?" I giggled.

"But you were... hell, somewhere, not here."

"I came back earlier. Tweeti picked me up from the airport. I had to take that time away from this and see what I truly wanted. I couldn't do what you or anybody else wanted. I had to do what I had to do. I want us, but I want a healthier more honest us."

He pulled me into his arms and kissed me all over my face. "Baby girl, I missed the fuck out of you. I thought I had lost you forever." He kissed me all over.

I hugged him tightly and kissed him on the lips. "You only lost me temporarily. I had to find myself because I had lost it for a minute. I want this, and I want us, Grizz. I just want you to be open and honest with me."

He laid me on my back and pulled my shirt over my head. My nipples were hard just looking at this man. He spread my legs and stuck his fingers in me and pulled out. He sucked all three of his fingers and smirked while looking me. I wanted this dick and craved it. He stood up and pulled his shorts off and then climbed between my legs and pushed himself inside of me. I moaned as I scratched his back and felt his width stretch me like it always did. Grizz looked me right in the eye as he continued to push deeper and deeper inside of me. I took my legs and wrapped them as best as I could around him. The strokes he gave me had my eyes rolling to the back of my head. He kissed my nipples as he continued to dick me down, then took one in his mouth. His tongue swished over my nipple and made me arch my back while he held my pelvis and continued to fuck the shit out of me.

My soul had come out and was staring at me from above. I smiled as he continued to bring me to my climax. Before I knew it, he flipped me on top of him and positioned me right how he wanted me. I stared down at him as he took one of my nipples between his fingers and played with it like it was dice or something.

"Ride this shit," he demanded.

I held onto his chest and rode him like my life depended on it. The way my ass jiggled while bouncing down on his dick had me turned on. "You like that..." I moaned as I continued to fuck the shit out of him. Months without sex would have you turning into a porn star.

"Like? Nah, I love this shit," he moaned and held me in place. We fucked each other until we both came and laid beside each other.

By the time we got done, the sun was coming up. We both were tired but could go another round if either of us wanted. It was like we craved each other's body and needed it as fuel. The way he pushed my hair out of my face as he looked down at me told me I had made the right decision. Grizz fucked up, and by fucking up, he fucked up so bad. Except, I knew his heart and, I knew he did what he did trying to help someone else out. Teyanna took advantage of his heart, and in the end, it backfired on him. I could spend my life blaming him, or I could forgive him and move on. That time of our life happened, we lived through it, and now we had to move on.

So many women liked to think they were forgiving and they weren't. Soon as that man did some shit they didn't like, they would be throwing the past right in his face. That wasn't forgiveness. In order to forgive, you had to be okay with what you were forgiving. You couldn't tell a man you forgave him and then a week later he forgot to take the trash out and you were screaming at him because he cheated on you six years ago. Bitterness was a hard pill to swallow, and I found myself crossing that line of bitter. To save myself, I needed to take a step back and look at this differently. I'd sat in therapy sessions since a kid, and they could never teach me what I had learned in the three months I spent alone. Therapy was a good tool, yet it just wasn't for me.

I needed him to understand that I forgave him and that I loved him. This was what I wanted, and I wanted to give us a try. I wasn't going to give us another chance; I wanted to just give us a chance.

"What are you doing?" I giggled as he pulled me from my thoughts. He was pushing me on my stomach.

"Get up on your knees," he demanded. I did what he told me and felt him pull my ass apart and felt his tongue in my butt.

"Ohh, Grizzz," I moaned out because the shit felt so good. I put face down in the pillow and screamed while enjoying what my man was doing to my body. My body *needed* this.

I SAT IN THE MIRROR AT MY VANITY AND APPLIED THE LAST coat of lip gloss on my lips. Checking my makeup, I was satisfied. It had been so long since I put makeup on and did my hair. Grizz must have been praying really hard that I would use my key. All my wigs were on doll heads waiting for me in my closet. My hands were itching to put one on, and I grabbed a jet black one and installed it. Running my hands through my lace front, I smiled because I looked so beautiful. Today was Paisley's baby shower. As much as she screamed to me over the phone that she just wanted a small brunch, none of us were hearing that. Tweeti and Manic had planned this whole baby shower. While she thought she was going to her favorite restaurant with a few friends, Shad had allowed us to use he and Emory's house to throw the baby shower. How Manic was going to get her to their house without asking questions was beyond me.

It had been a week since I had been back in the states and living with Grizz again. I told Paisley about everything, and she was so happy for me. It seemed like everyone was rooting for me and Grizz to get back together. She told me that she and Manic were going to move in together into his condo before Aubree was born. Manic's condo was bigger than the one me and Paisley were living in, so it made perfect sense. With her being close to delivery, they needed to finally get things for Aubree in order. I was just excited to celebrate her and Aubree today. This had been a long pregnancy, and she had worried her entire pregnancy about the baby. Now was the time for her to sit back and relax so she could enjoy us celebrating her.

"You ready? The car's downstairs waiting for us." Grizz came into the bathroom while fastening his Rolex around his wrist. He stood behind me and stared as if he was admiring me. "Damn, you're so beautiful," he complimented me, and I blushed.

"Thank you. Let me just spray some perfume, grab my purse, and slip into my heels, and we can go," I told him as I stood up from the chair.

Once I stood up, he pulled me close to him and kissed me

on the lips. Thankfully, the lip gloss I was using was matte. "I don't know how many times I have to say it or how much, but I want to thank you for giving me another chance, baby. You're my entire world. I've always said you were important to me, but almost losing you taught me just how important you are to me."

I looked into his eyes and kissed him on the lips. "If we don't have trust, we don't have anything. I want you to know that I'll believe whatever you say, long as you do the same for me."

"You got my word." He kissed me once more before he slapped my ass, as I walked away to go grab the things I needed to finish getting ready.

We held hands as we walked out of the building, and the door was opened by our personal chauffer. When I climbed into the back, I started smiling because I saw Jah and Tweeti there.

"Look at you looking like your old self. I didn't want to say anything, but you was looking like a damn hippy last week," she joked. "I love this dress." She touched the long flowy Dolce and Gabbana maxi dress that I wore. I paired it with a pair of pumps and had a blazer over it because it was chilly.

"And Grizz has my hat." I pointed at the hat that was a part of the dress code for the baby shower.

"I'm excited for Paisley to see everything. I was at Shad and Emory's house until late last night, then I had to go bring Paris her dress because she had it shipped to my damn house by accident."

"How did she do it by accident?"

"It's Paris. Do you really need to ask that question?" We all laughed because we knew how Paris was. She was a teenager, and nothing revolving her made any sense.

WE PULLED UP TO THE CIRCULAR DRIVEWAY OF SHAD AND Emory's estate. Each time I visited this house, it reminded me just how powerful my friends were. Uzi and Jah were just regular to me. They were like big brothers that I never wanted. The doors were opened by the butlers who dressed in three-piece suits. I stepped out and walked into the house. Tweeti had outdone herself with the decorations. The theme was Aubree and Wonderland. Everything was Alice and Wonderland themed, but instead of Alice, it was replaced with Aubree. Since Paisley wanted a brunch kind of theme, they kept to that tradition but had a huge table with finger foods, drinks, and desserts. This setup was so beautiful, and I just knew Paisley was going to love it. A waiter handed me a glass of champagne, and I took it as me and Grizz made our way around the house. The gift table was already filled with so many gifts.

"Sundae, how are you, gorgeous?" I heard Emory's voice from behind me. Turning around, I smiled and looked at her. She was dressed in a satin green colored dressed that stopped below her knees, nude Versace pumps, and jewelry that caused me to squint when she came near for a hug.

"I'm doing great. How are you doing?"

She whipped her left hand out and showed her ring finger. "Shad just upgraded my ring again. You know we're planning a wedding again." She gloated. It was typical Emory fashion to brag on what was new in her life.

"Wow, that's amazing. I hope I receive an invitation."

"We're doing it on a yacht on the coast of Italy, so of course you'll be invited." She smiled. "This man of mines just wants to keep me happy. You know the building he bought for him and the boys? Well, it's worth millions with the work that they have put into it," she continued.

"Amazing. Anything that Shad touches turns to gold."

"Ain't that right. We're also considering moving overseas

and getting a compound there too. You know... he's just trying to keep me this time."

Tweeti informed me about his new mistress who was tired of playing second. Jah had told her how their father wanted to end things with Emory again and they told him to make sure it was what he wanted to do. I guess he didn't have the heart or pockets to break her heart again because they were still together. Emory was so blind to it all that she didn't notice that her husband was gone more than he was home. Like now, Shad was away on business, and she was here hosting alone. If those rings and trips were able to make her turn a blind eye, who was I to bring it up?

"I guess he is... Did Remi arrive?"

"Yes, she's here. I think she's hungover or something. Keeps vomiting. I told her I have some important people here from the country club attending so she better get it together." She pursed her lips.

I now understood why Wynner was such a tight ass. What was sad was that Wynner wasn't always like that. We never invited her to go out because she acted like she was the mother of the group. If I wanted to go hang out with my mother, I would invite her. In fact, my mother would probably be more turned up than Wynner was. All she did was check her phone, FaceTime her husband, and talk about the kids. The dynamic of our friendship changed, and I hated it.

"Let me go and check on her... I'll talk to you in a bit."

"Thank you, Sundae. The extra weight on you looks amazing," she complimented, kissed me on the cheek, and patted my shoulder as she walked over to her next victim who had to listen to all her bragging.

Once I found the bathroom, I knocked on it a few times before I heard Remi's voice. I turned the knob and quickly entered the bathroom. "Rem, you okay?"

Me and Rem didn't really talk while I was away. We talked

once, and that was that. She was going through a lot, and I didn't want to push into her life unless she wanted me there. I also knew it had a lot to do with what her and Tweeti were going through too.

"Dae, you look so beautiful. Girl, I've missed you." She smiled weakly as she laid slumped over the toilet bowl.

"A golden toilet bowl... Who does that?"

"Emory McKnight wouldn't have anything less," she mocked in Emory's voice. "Girl, I feel like shit, but I needed to be here for Paisley."

"You were drinking or something? Emory told me that you were hungover."

"I'm pregnant and haven't told anyone except Tweeti. Emory always assumes the worst about someone. Why couldn't I just be sick?"

"Well, you know that's Emory."

I helped her up from the floor and fixed her dress. Digging in my purse, I found some of my perfume and sprayed her. "Thank you. All the food is making me feel sick to my stomach."

"Morning sickness is kicking your ass."

"Uh huh, and these ginger candies I bought online aren't working at all."

"Uzi doesn't know?"

"Not yet. We're supposed to talk later tonight. I told him he could drive me home tonight and we can talk," she explained as she washed her face and hands.

"Why haven't you told him sooner?"

"Fear. I guess I'm scared that he's going to want to put the wedding back on, move me back into the brownstone, and all those other things just because I'm pregnant. I shouldn't have been kicked out or the wedding shouldn't have been called off because I said I didn't want to have kids. He made me feel like I was useless to him and disposable."

"You have to remember people have their own way on how they deal with things. Maybe that was his way of trying to deal with something that was hard for him to process."

"Just because I'm having this baby doesn't mean that I'm moving back home with him. I'm still going to stay in the condo, and we can co-parent while working toward building a relationship again."

"I'll pray for you two. I know he loves the hell out of you."

"And I love him. Sometimes love isn't enough."

"Don't I know it."

She looked over at me and smiled. "Love was enough because you and Grizz are back together I heard."

"We are. I just needed to see what I wanted."

"Getting away helped you to see that?"

Nodding my head, I fixed my hair in the mirror. "I cut him out of my life for three months and just focused on me and my needs. Grizz crossed my mind occasionally, but I had to push him out of my mind. When it was all said and done, when I was coming home, he was all that was on my mind. I wore the key he gave me the entire three months and thought about what I wanted, not what he wanted."

"I'm glad that you were able to get away and clear your mind. I should probably do the same thing."

"Yeah, like Uzi gonna let you go away with his baby in your belly."

"You're right." She laughed.

"You good in here?"

"Now I am." She hugged me.

We headed back out to the shower, and everyone was standing around talking while eating the finger foods or drinking the champagne that was being served. We found Tweeti in the kitchen telling the caterer how to position the deviled eggs.

"Stop being bossy and try to enjoy the party," Remi advised.

"I know. I just want to make sure everything is perfect. Then I have Emory getting on my damn nerves about small shit," she stressed.

"I know you used her house, but why is she even here?"

"She wasn't going to miss this party. If a party is going down, she's going to be here." Remi grabbed some ginger ale out of the fridge and drank it straight out the bottle. "Whew, this shit burns."

"Paton is here." Emory came into the kitchen in a rush. We looked at her like she was crazy because we didn't know who she was talking about. "Why are you all stuck on stupid?"

"Who the hell is Paton?" I asked and looked at both Tweeti and Remi. They were just as confused as me.

"This damn girl's shower," she elaborated.

"It's Paisley, Emory." Tweeti cut her eyes at her and rushed past her. We all made it to the foyer as she and Manic were walking into the house. Paisley was looking around the house in awe. When she noticed us, she walked over and hugged all of us.

"Thank you so much. I love it all."

"You haven't seen anything yet. Come into the house more." Tweeti took her by the hand and showed her around.

All you heard was her gasping at everything Tweeti showed her. "Who is all these people?" Paisley wondered. She didn't have much family or friends beside us.

"Emory invited all her rich friends, so you gonna have some good gifts or cash."

"Oh..." She allowed her voice to trail off as she smiled at people she had no clue who they were.

The party was in full swing, and everyone was enjoying themselves. I was drinking a virgin drink and sitting by

Paisley as she smiled when someone came up to her and handed her an envelope filled with a gift card or cash. Manic was talking with the guys, and Tweeti was with Remi trying to make sure everything went perfect.

"This shower is so beautiful." Wynner came over with a drink in her hand and her youngest daughter holding on to her leg.

"Thank you. I appreciate you for coming."

"I appreciate the invitation. My mother wasn't going to let me not attend an event happening at our family's home." She smiled. "Sundae! When did you get back?"

"Last week."

"We need to do lunch so you can fill me in on everything." She smiled and reached down to kiss me on the cheek.

Qua came over and kissed Paisley on the cheek and slipped her an envelope filled with money. You could tell from how thick the envelope was that there was money in it. "Congratulations, mama."

"Thank you. I appreciate it." Paisley smiled and set the envelope with the stack of others. Because of who Manic was, you saw nothing but hood niggas coming up to her and handing her money. Emory was pissed because they were invited, but who told her to invite all these snobby people who didn't want to interact with anyone except the people they knew at the party.

"Are you going to do a nanny or do everything yourself?"

"Well, I work from home, so I'm not going to do a nanny. If I decide to go back to work, I will probably have Ms. Evelyn watch the baby."

"Tweeti's mama?"

"Yes. She's good with Taz."

Wynner leaned in. "You do know her mother used to be a dr—"

"Wynner!" I sternly shouted lowly.

"What? She should know who she is leaving her child with."

"This isn't the time nor the place to discuss all of that," I warned her. Paisley didn't need to know any of that right now.

"Well, we should do play dates. I have two girls, and I know you already have a daughter around the same age as mine."

"Sure thing." Paisley smiled. Wynner hugged her and walked away with that baby looking terrified at everyone while she held onto her mother's leg. Qua walked away quickly after he handed that money off. I hated to say it, but she and Qua were going to be like Emory and Shad a couple years down the line.

"What is her problem?" Paisley asked.

"Girl, generational curse." I rolled my eyes.

"I'm a little sad that you're moving out." She reached out and grabbed ahold of my hand. "I'm gonna miss coming in your room when I need something."

"Me too. Now I have to drive a few blocks down to your house just to see you." I sulked. She smirked but looked away. "Bitch, spill."

"Well, you didn't hear it from me, but we're moving to your building on the floor below you guys. There's only one penthouse apartment in that building, and you guys got it, but our new place is bigger than Manic's old condo."

"Are you fucking serious? Why didn't you tell me?"

"Manic told me to be quiet about it." She smirked. "Now that it's official, we can talk about it."

"You know this has nothing to do with us, right?"

"Oh, I know. Grizz and Manic can't be too far from each other." She laughed. "I'm just excited you'll be upstairs so you can come down and help me with these kids."

"Oh, you already know I'll be there to help you." I smiled and stood up to hug her.

I never expected that me and Paisley would develop a bond the way we did. This woman had been through so much and failed by so many people, but her love and heart were still there. She would give the shirt off her back to anyone who asked. I loved that she loved hard, despite everything she had been through. In the end, she loved everyone and just wanted to be loved in return. Here she was raising the daughter of the man that abused her for years. You didn't meet anybody with a heart that pure. It was because of her heart that she was blessed the way she was.

"What my baby mama over here doing?" Manic came over and kissed Paisley before rubbing her swollen stomach.

"Telling Sundae about the new place." She smiled with a bright smile. You could tell the love the both of them shared was genuine and that Manic loved the hell out of this woman.

"Yo, you got a big mouth." He kissed her on the cheek. "You hype you about to be living near her again?" He turned his attention to me.

"Yeah. I loved living with her. Don't be surprised when I'm up in y'all bed venting in the middle of the night."

"And don't be surprised when a snake wrap around your leg either."

"The hell?" I looked at him weird.

"He sleeps nude, and he's always hard." Paisley rolled her eyes.

"Eww, that's fucking nasty. I'll just come when he's not around, period."

"I mean, soon as she drops Aubree, we fucking all over... so Aubree and Sayana might be downstairs at your crib."

"Are you kidding me?"

"Dead ass... I got my dream girl, and we haven't fucked since she got pregnant. Nah, my dick about to get real wet."

"You do know I can't have sex for six weeks after I have

Aubree, right?" Paisley reminded him. When she said it, he had this glazed over look like he didn't give a damn.

"You do know soon as they take her to the nursery in the hospital I'm fucking you, right?" Me and Paisley looked at him like he was crazy. "On a serious note, thank you for taking my nigga back. All this nigga do is smile now."

"I didn't do it for him. I did it for me." I smiled.

He smiled, kissed Paisley once more, and then went back over to the guys. Me and Paisley continued talking on how we were going to decorate Aubree's nursery and all the things we would do when she was born.

"Can I ask you a serious question?" she asked and looked me right in the eye.

"Yeah, what's up?"

"Will you be Aubree's godmother?"

When she asked, I had to take a doubletake to see if she was serious. When I realized that she was serious, I jumped up and hugged her tightly. "I would be so honored to be your daughter's godmother."

"Good, because we already made her middle name Sundae." She laughed, and tears came to my eyes.

"Stop getting me all emotional, Paisley."

"I'm really not trying to, but you've been here for me more than I could ever thank you for. Even with you being all over the world, you made time to call me every Sunday to check in with me. Even with you going through your own personal issues, you still wanted to drag me out the house and make me feel better. Small stuff like that doesn't go unnoticed to me. When I needed a friend, you were there. Don't get me wrong, all of you girls welcomed me in and I appreciate that. However, I think me and you formed a deeper bond."

"Girl, I love you and saw how broken you were. When I went through my miscarriage, you sat in that bathtub with me and held me naked while I cried and asked God what was wrong with me? You've been there for me when I really needed someone."

We both were an emotional wreck. When we noticed some of Emory's friends staring at us, we wiped our faces and laughed. "I love you, friend." She held my hand.

"I love you too, friend." I smiled back as I squeezed her hand.

As the baby shower came to an end, Paisley had over twenty thousand dollars in cash and a shit load of gifts. Manic had to go rent a small U-Haul just so they could get everything packed in the truck to bring to their new crib. Both Manic and Paisley thanked everyone before they left. Tweeti was taking Sayana for the night because Manic had a special night planned for the both of them before Aubree came. I stood on the balcony looking over the McKnight estate.

"You had a good time tonight?" I felt Grizz's cool breath on my neck. Along with the coolness of his breath, I could smell the rum he had been drinking while talking with the guys.

"I did. Paisley was so excited about everything. I'm glad that we were able to get her excited about the baby."

"I heard she told you something too."

I spun around in his arms and faced him. "She did. Why you didn't tell me? What happened to no secrets?"

"Bad secrets. This one was a good one."

"I'll give you a pass this time." I reached up and kissed him on the lips.

"Let's get out of here and go home."

"Home... I like the sound of that." I put my hand in his, and we headed out of the house. Home was where the heart was. I just needed to figure out if that was where I wanted to be. Once I did, I found home with Grizz.

✺ 17 ✺

UZI

It was late, and I didn't feel like driving all the way to the city to drop Remi home and then going home. When my mother told me that Remi fell asleep in the guest suite, I took that as my sign to stay the night. My mother told the cleaning service where to put everything and retired upstairs to her bedroom. I knew once she closed herself in her room, she wouldn't be out for a minute. Tomorrow was Manic's dad shower that he insisted that we throw him. We took it as a joke, but this nigga cut us off for two weeks because we hadn't planned shit. So we got a section at the strip club and decided we would drink, toss money, and bullshit. When I thought about it, the nigga did need a damn dad shower because he was having two damn kids. Nisha was due any day with their baby.

To set him up for fatherhood, we were going to smoke some green, chill, and catch up since we hadn't done that in a while. Everyone was invited, even J-Rell. Manic was pissed because he still didn't like him, but tomorrow was for the guys, and we were going to chill. I fixed me a small plate and headed to the guest suite where Remi was sleeping. I didn't give a fuck that we weren't together or that we hadn't slept in the same bed in months. Tonight, she was about to sleep in the same bed as me. Shit, the bed was a California king bed anyway. When I entered the room, I was smacking on some little cucumber sandwich with mayo on it. The shit was small but was good as hell.

When I asked Tweeti why she didn't have real baby shower food, she told me to blame my mother. Evelyn was going to cook everything from baked macaroni and cheese to ribs and everything in between, but my mother stopped it because she said this wasn't a baby shower being thrown in a project community center. Sometimes I had to stop myself from checking my moms because she seemed to forget we came from the projects and that we didn't always have money. Since it was too late to find another venue, Tweeti said she sucked it up and hired the caterer that my mother used for all her dinner parties.

Me and Tweeti were in a better place these days. I admit, she made my ass get in line when it came to her husband. As the nigga that has always held this family down, she made me see that my little brother didn't need me anymore. She damn sure made me check myself on disregarding her as his wife. I had watched my father do it to my moms so much that I started doing the shit to women. Remi told me that I did it to her, and she didn't like it. I agreed just so she could shut up and move on, but I saw that was an issue I needed to work on. It was an issue that I needed to address so that my next relationship wouldn't be toxic. The last thing I wanted was for some nigga to treat my daughter that way. I exited out the bedroom and went back to the kitchen to grab my phone off the counter. My mother was back in the kitchen with her silk robe pouring a glass of chardonnay.

"Mama, what you doing back up?"

"I never went to sleep." Her eyes were red, and I could tell she had been crying. "You okay, sweetie?"

"Ma, what's wrong?" She couldn't fake the funk with me. I could see she had been crying, and she probably thought everyone was asleep, so she slipped down here to grab a glass of wine.

Sniffling, she put on that smile that told me she was about to lie. "Baby boy, I'm fine. Go get some sleep. Manic was telling me all about his little event tomorrow."

"Nah, tell me what is going on?"

"Parrish, you really don't need to worry about anything."

"Ma, you can either tell me now... or I'm gonna ask when everyone's around." I knew she was about to tell me because she would be mortified if I asked in front of everyone. My mother was the type that her entire world could be crashing down, but to save face, she would keep a smile on her face and then behind closed doors, break down alone. She had always been like that, and as she got older, I wished she would stop.

Sighing, she sat down at the kitchen island and took a sip of her wine. "Your father is having an affair."

It was something I already knew, but I wasn't going to speak on it to her. I learned a long time ago not to get involved with my parent's personal shit. "How did you find out?"

She waved her hand and took another sip of her wine. "I found out months ago. She's not the issue because she knows her place. I'm more pissed with your father. He has bought her a brand-new home in Jersey," she revealed to me nonchalantly.

"Wait, you mad because he bought her a brand-new home?"

"Um, yes. Are you paying attention? She's a whore and is to stay in her place. He promised me that she'll always be second to me, but he couldn't attend today's event because he had to help her pick out furniture for her new place."

I felt so sad for my mother. Did she not know that even at her golden age that she was beautiful? My mother was in her late forties and looked like she was in her twenties. Black didn't crack, and she could still pass for the girls that were around my age. Why was she settling for a man that couldn't love just her? My father could never just love her; he always had to have someone else too. I understood that he wanted to be happy, but he should have let my mother be when they divorced. Instead, he couldn't take that she was happy and living life on her terms. My father was that nigga that when his girl started losing weight, getting her confidence up, he would go and get her ass pregnant. Old creep ass nigga. Still, I loved my old man, just hated his ways and how he did my mother.

"Ma, why do you put up with this?"

"Look around here. You see the house; you see everything that I have? Do you think I would give this up to have another woman in my castle living like me? When I lived alone for those months, I lived well, but did I live like this? I had to worry about paying this or that, and here, I just float around while your father and his accountants handle all the money. I still sit on a good lump of cash and get to spend your father's money." She chuckled and polished off the rest of her wine. "Oh, while I continue to have my affair with my twenty-seven year old trainer." She winked.

"Word? Ma, you getting down like that?"

"My grandkids will know they come from a family of love. They will spend holidays with their grandparents and think the world of us. They don't have to know that we live secret lives behind closed doors."

"Ma, you know Paris is old enough to figure things out."

"The day she figures out what is going on is the day me and her will sit down with tea and have a conversation. Until then, I'm going to continue to live life the way it works for me."

"Ight, Mama." I sighed. My mother had her mind made up that this was going to work for her and my father. It was going to work until his side bitch got tired of coming second. It could be next month or a few years from now, but she was going to get tired of coming second and want more from her relationship with Shad McKnight.

"I love you, baby." She kissed me on the cheek before she retreated back upstairs to her bedroom.

I grabbed my phone feeling more mind fucked than ever. My parents had the weirdest shit ever going on. As much as I told them and myself that I didn't want to be involved, I was always somehow dragged into their shit. When I made it back to the guestroom, Remi wasn't in the bed. I heard dry heaving in the bathroom and tossed my phone on the bed and went into the bathroom. When I opened the door, I found her sitting on the floor near the toilet. She had tears in her eyes, and her face was red as fuck.

"You good?" I asked and went and sat beside her.

She was catching her breathing and nodded her head yes. "I thought you would have gone home," she spoke when she had finally caught her breath.

"Nah, it didn't make sense. Plus, I wanted to make sure you got home straight tomorrow. What you ate that got you this sick?"

"Dick."

"The fuck, Remi?"

"Your dick got me sick like this." She rolled her eyes.

"I know I got some dope dick, but damn, it got yo... Don't play with me, Rem. You not telling me what I think you're telling me." I jumped to my feet and looked at her with a smile on my face.

She had this little smile on her face. "I'm pregnant... again," she revealed. "And before you ask, I'm keeping it."

"Yoooooooo! Yeahhhhhhhhh! Fuck, man! Thank you, God!" I jumped up and down and hollered.

"I have a headache from throwing up. Can we pipe down on the screaming?"

"My bad... when this happened?"

"I found out last month. I've been trying to find out how or when I was going to tell you," she admitted.

"Last month? Rem, you got checked out and shit?"

"Yeah, I went, and that's how I found out. The doctor said I'm fine," she informed me. "I have another appointment coming up. He promised we can do an ultrasound this visit."

I got down on the floor and looked into her eyes. "Baby, we gotta make this work."

"No, we're not going to make this work because I'm having this baby. I want to make this work because you want and love me. You kicked me out what I thought was our home because of my own right and decision."

The way she said it made me realize that shit wasn't right. She didn't have to have a baby; that was her right and choice. I couldn't help that I was in my feelings and saw my relationship going down the wrong path. We were arguing about stupid shit, and the vibe in the house was off. It was time for one of us to go, and being that I caught her looking up apartments on her laptop, I made the decision to give her the push she clearly wanted or needed.

"You right. I did push you out, and I apologize about that."

"Uzi, I understand that you wanted a baby, but you treated me like a fucking baby maker, not a woman. You didn't once ask why I didn't want to have a baby or try to find out the reason. Instead, you shut me out because things weren't going your way. I know I have my selfish ways and I'm a work in progress, but the way you moved was selfish as well. Just because I'm having your baby doesn't mean we're back together, getting married, or even moving in together again. Just like you were quick to show me the door, you need to win my heart back." She set the ground rules. I had to respect what she was saying.

Holding her hands, I kissed them. "Bet. If I gotta win you back, you already know I'm competitive as hell, and I don't lose."

"Suit up, then." She smirked and then gagged. Holding her hair, I watched and gagged as she threw up the shit she ate today at the shower.

If I had to win her back, then that was what I was going to do. She was right; we ended because I wanted it to happen, and I even showed her ass the door. I had a lot of flaws with myself that I had to work on as well, and the fact that she wasn't falling back into my hands like putty let me know that she wasn't about to put up with my shit. All I could do was be there for her and make sure she and my soon to be baby was straight, all while trying to win her heart back. By now, I thought we would have been married already, but life had a way of humbling you. I was taking the challenge, and I was going to get my woman back.

"NIGGA, WHY YOU GOT THAT SHIRT ON?" JAH LAUGHED AS Manic walked around our section with a shirt that read *I got two baby mamas and they know about each other.*

"Hell yeah. You already know I had to show out. In fact, I got y'all niggas shirts too, but they in my car," he replied and poured some D'USSÉ into his cup.

"I'm not wearing no damn shirt," Jah protested.

"Yeah, me either, and I know you didn't get my right size," Grizz added.

"Y'all niggas are boring as fuck. Anyway, I'm glad that you were all able to make it, except you, J-Rell." We all shook our heads because the nigga J-Rell held his drink up and nodded his head. He knew that Manic didn't like his ass, and he didn't try and force a relationship with the nigga.

"It's all love, Manic." He laughed.

"Not over here, nigga." Manic got serious.

"Can we focus on the task at hand." I brought him back from that crazed ass look he got when he was mad. "You about to be a father to two. I'm about to be a father for the second time."

"Word? Rem pregnant?" Jah asked.

"Yeah, she told me last night."

"Nah, I'm mad happy for you two. I know this was what you wanted. All you niggas having babies and shit... I need to go put one in Sundae."

"Chill. You just got your girl back. Focus on the two of you, not trying to have a baby," Jah advised, and I agreed with him.

"You right," Grizz also agreed with him. "Shit's been amazing. I been fucking since she used that key." He smirked. This nigga was happy as fuck now that he got Sundae back in his life.

Teyanna's body was burned with dog remains. We had a nigga that worked at a pet cemetery, and he cremated the body for us with somebody's dog. She was no longer an issue in his life, and if you asked me, the nigga been should have ended the shit between them and popped that bitch. You only had one time to cross me, and you could kiss your ass goodbye.

"I'm glad for you, man. 'Cause if you walked around being

depressed one more time, I was going to have to tell you about yourself," Manic joked.

"Shut the fuck up." I laughed.

"Yerrrr, Peblo, come on over!" Manic yelled to Peblo who had just walked in. Peblo had disappeared and nobody heard from him.

When he did turn back up, he had gotten himself clean and was trying to change his life around. That man was a good man and had lost his way for a while. After speaking to my pops, I was able to get him to rent him an apartment in his new building. Then I was able to get him to work at a few of our properties as a maintenance man. Who knew that the nigga was so handy? Just like I was the nigga supplying the drugs that was destroying our communities, I could also be the one making a change in my community too. Just like I served Peblo and helped in his demise, I could lend a hand in helping him with his success. It was how I slept at night.

"Hey, fellas!" he greeted. "Glad to see you're back up on your feet, boss." He nodded at Jah.

"Appreciate you, Peblo. What you doing here?" Jah asked him.

"I wash dishes here in the back on the weekends. You know, have to keep the money rolling in. You and your family have done so much for me, but at the end of the day, I'm a man, and I have to provide for myself."

"That's why you a real one, P!" Grizz raised his glass to him.

"Yeah, on that note, I'm about to head out. When y'all praising a damn *crackhead* , I know the drinks been hitting." J-Rell laughed and dapped everyone except Manic before he left.

I noticed Peblo's face. It was as if he'd just seen a ghost take a shit on the table. He stood there and tried three times to snap out of it but couldn't. We all noticed how he was acting and looked at each other.

"You good, P?" Grizz asked.

"Y... yeah, I'm good," he stammered and tried to walk away, but Manic stepped in front of him. "I really should get to work."

"Not until you tell us why you look like a transsexual slapped you in the face with their dick," he told him.

"Out of all the things to use, you use that shit?" I asked.

Manic shrugged. Peblo wiped the sweat that accumulated on his forehead. "That's the man that shot you. Why are you hanging around him?" Peblo questioned Jah.

"Wait, what? Nah, Peblo, you bugging." Jah waved it off.

"When he shot you, he said 'who would believe a crack-head?' I *know* that voice, and I've heard it replay in my head every day since you were shot. His words were the reason I got clean. It was because it was true. Who would believe me, a crackhead, in anything?"

"You telling us that J-Rell was the one who shot Jah?" Manic asked again so we could understand exactly what he was saying.

"Money. There was money, and he loaded his car up with money and left the scene."

When Peblo mentioned the money, I knew that he was telling me the truth. We had never recovered the missing money from the trap, and the cops I had on the force said they never recovered money, just some drugs. I wasn't worried about the drugs because we were going to re-up the next day on product, which was why all the money was being picked up the night before.

"Peblo, you telling me J-Rell shot my brother?" I asked one more time with hate laced in my voice. This entire time I was still breaking bread with the enemy. This nigga visited Jah in the hospital knowing that he tried to murk him and that he stole from my family.

"Boss, he tried to kill Jah." How could I not believe this man? He was shaking and damn near in tears telling me that J-Rell was the nigga that tried to kill my brother.

"He took money out the family's mouth and tried to take Jah out... I want him dead."

"When boss said get 'em, we gon' get 'em." Manic growled and put his drink down, ready to go to war.

✺ 18 ✺

These niggas must have been the stupidest hustlers that I had ever run across. I tried to kill their own and then robbed them, yet they were still inviting me to chill and were breaking bread with me. It was so hard to be around Uzi without laughing at the fool he was. This man was the king of Harlem and hadn't figured out that I was the nigga that tried to kill his brother and robbed his ass. When the crackhead that witnessed me shooting Jah came through, I wasn't worried. He probably didn't remember because his ass was cracked out or something. To keep him from not remembering, I got out of there. Part of me got out there quick because I couldn't stand that rainbow haired nigga. If anybody was going to figure me out, it was going to be that nigga. He was always questioning me and shit, and a few times, I caught him in the same area that I was in.

When I walked through the door of my home, I shook my head. The sound of crying, smell of cigarette smoke, and hollering was what welcomed me. Dakota had gotten kicked out of Jah's condo and had nowhere to go. I started to take the baby then thought about having to care for my son all alone. Dallas was in Miami at our new condo. She told me that I needed to close things out here and join her because she was done with New York. All the money was down there with her, and she was investing the money the right way. We would be opening up a little restaurant and shit to make some legit money. I even met some zoe niggas down there that were gonna give me some bricks on consignment once I got there.

The reason I was still here was because I couldn't just dip. I planned on telling Uzi that I needed a change and wanted to move to Miami. I was going to see if he offered me the position of expanding down there. Once I found out his connect, it would be over for that nigga. When I walked into the living room, Dakota was sitting in front of the TV with a cigarette in one hand and the baby in the other, watching *Jeopardy*. The bitch didn't do anything with herself except sit in this house and smoke packs of cigarettes. Then she didn't even smoke the real ones; she smoked the seven-dollar packs that gave you headaches.

"How was the little event?" she asked and looked my way. "You could act like you want to hold your son. Been in this house all day watching this boy."

"As his mot—"

"As his father, you should do the same things that I'm doing. Except, you're not. You lucky my friend Lucy coming over to get him."

Lucy was a lady that lived in the building who watched everyone's kid. She was a sweet Asian lady who couldn't have kids of her own. If she told me the shit one more time when she came to pick my son up, I was going to tell her to keep my damn son. Dakota took advantage and had that lady watching our son even when she didn't have anything to do.

"Good... I had some drinks and want some pussy and head."

Soon as she heard that I wanted to fuck her and get my dick sucked, she got so excited she damn near fucking dropped our son. "Soon as Lucy bring her ass, I'm gonna shower, brush my teeth, and it's on."

Fucking Dakota while my wife was in Miami setting our life together was fucked up, but at the end of the day, I needed to relieve some stress. It wasn't like we didn't all used to fuck together, so it didn't count as cheating. Dakota thought she had the best pussy, and that was far from the truth. Her shit was all loose, and she didn't know how to throw that shit back. Her ass was all stiff and shit. Dallas knew how to fuck daddy's dick good, and that was why I missed the shit out of my wife.

Like promised, Lucy came and scooped Aspen up and packed up a little bag for him. She said tomorrow she would take him to the park before bringing him home. I laid in the bed with my dick standing at attention while Dakota tried to twerk. I wasn't gonna lie; her little off rhythm ass had me turned on from all the twerking she was doing. When she was finally finished shaking her ass, she came over and devoured my dick in one gulp. It hit the back of her throat a few times and she didn't gag once. The way she sucked my dick had my toes curled. With my eyes closed and my arms behind my back, all you heard was her slurping up my dick.

"Come bounce on this dick," I demanded and kept my eyes closed. She did as she was told and eased down on my dick and went crazy on my shit. Sex with Dakota was medi-ocre, but tonight, she was throwing it down on my dick. It was like she had something to prove to me tonight.

"Daddy, this dick feels so good in my pussy," she moaned. That was another thing I hated about her. She always felt the need to narrate what the fuck was going on. Bitch, I didn't need you to narrate. I needed you to take all this dick and be quiet and give me an occasional moan to let me know I was doing good with performance.

"Yeah, shut up and take this dick," I demanded and reached up and choked her while pumping into her while she continued to bounce up and down on my dick. "Ride this dick while I take a nap."

"Okay, baby," she agreed like I knew she would.

With my eyes closed, I enjoyed her silently riding my dick while I thought about my life. Miami was about to be a fucking movie. My baby was down there setting shit up, and I was about to be ghost. What I was trying to figure out was if I was going to bring my son with me or leave him with his mother. This place was paid up until the end of the year, so she needed to find her another nigga to leech off of, because I was going to be gone.

"Yeah, ride this nigga's dick... oh shit, oh shit, I'm about to cum." I heard a male's voice, and my eyes popped open. Manic was laughing like a fucking maniac. I always thought they called him Manic because of his hair, but looking at how this nigga laughed and carried himself, he was a fucking maniac.

When I opened my eyes, I was looking right into Manic's homicidal eyes. He put his multicolored grills in, and his hair wasn't in the bun it was in earlier. He had it out wild while he ran his tongue across those colorful ass grills.

"What's popping, blood?" He nodded his head and continued to look me in the eyes. I looked to my left, and Grizz was sitting in the chair. I was so focused on Manic that I hadn't noticed that he had his hand tightly around Dakota's neck, and she was turning blue.

"What the fuck? Nigga, I know we ain't on no friendly shit, but why the fuck you in my crib? Let go of her," I told him, and he smiled.

Turning his head from side to side, he smiled at me.

"Hmmm, I'm thinking of a word. Guess the word, and I'll let her go." He continued to squeeze tighter and tighter. This bitch was looking like the little bitch from Willy Wonka that ate that damn gum and turned blue. My dick was now limp, and I was wondering what the hell was about to go on. When he was done, he released her, and she fell to the side and choked out this agonizing scream that could barely be heard. Her voice was now hoarse, and she kept grabbing at her throat as if she wanted to pull it off.

"You tried to kill Jah?" Grizz spoke in this low voice.

"Hell yeah... nigga tried to off me, and I'm still fucking rolling." Jah rolled in the room with Uzi trailing behind him with a phone to his ear.

"Nah, nah... Why the fuck would I do that?"

"Hold on." Uzi held his hand up to silence me. "What you said, shorty?"

"He tried to kill your brother and has me with all the money down here. I didn't know until my sister told me last week." I heard my fucking wife snitching on me like we didn't fucking have vows or plan this shit out together.

"Ight, bet... put my nigga back on the line."

"Yo, boss."

"Get rid of the trash."

"Done." It didn't take a rocket scientist to know that he was about to have someone kill Dallas. I was sad, then again, I wasn't, because that bitched dimed me out.

"What the fuck is going on, Uzi?" Here I was laying in the bed with a limp dick and a crazy nigga staring down at me like he was ready to kill my ass soon as he got the word.

"You came for the wrong family. Let me tell you something. You don't go against the McKnight family and live to talk about it. Yeah, we wasn't hip to your bullshit, but like Karma, it comes around, and now look where your ass at? Caught with your pants down... literally."

"Man, I don't know what you mean... Let me get us a beer and talk."

"Nah, we done talking." Jah turned and rolled out the room. Uzi followed behind him, and I was left behind with Grizz and Manic looking at me like fucking maniacs.

✼ 19 ✼

A ROSE IN HARLEM

P aris

"*A BROOKLYN MAN HAS BEEN FOUND DECAPITATED AND stuffed inside a mattress outside of Brown Reality office this morning. The entire block is cut off, and the real estate office is closed for the remainder of the week. We're unsure why this man was killed and brought to this exact place. The investigation is still in process. Diana, back to you.*"

"Yo, why you always watching the news?" Boo, one of my father's workers asked me.

I was home alone, like always, and watching the news while doing my homework. Ever since they skipped me a grade and put me in twelfth grade, I was studying and working ten times harder to keep my GPA up. At the start of the school year, I was talking, not paying attention, and the school reached out to my father. Instead of my father going up there, Remi came and sat in my class to try and clown me and make me pay attention. All I did was try to hold a conversation with her. It was then she realized that I wasn't paying attention because I was bored. All the shit they were teaching, I already knew, and was tired of learning the same shit over again. She spoke to the school's head mistress, and she didn't want to lose all the money my dad paid for tuition, so she agreed to try me out for a month in a twelfth-grade class. When I aced every test, assignment, and homework, they realized that I knew what the hell I was talking about.

They moved my class, and that was when I wished Remi didn't. Now that I was in twelfth grade at sixteen, almost seventeen, trying to juggle having a social life, school, and college applications, I felt like my head was spinning in every direction. The one thing I was excited about was that I had got accepted into Spellman College in Atlanta and Columbia University. I hadn't told my father yet because he had been preoccupied with he and Remi's relationship and the new baby that was on the way. I wasn't jealous but happy that I was finally going to be out of the spotlight. There were other colleges that I applied to, but those were the best offers. I didn't have to worry about tuition because my father would cover that. I hadn't decided if I wanted to move away or if I wanted to stay in New York City. If I did, I knew I needed my own place because living with my father while trying to be a college student wasn't going to work for me.

"Yo, baby, you gonna come through to my crib?" Boo asked, and I smiled because he knew I was. My birthday was next week, and I couldn't wait to be seventeen so I didn't hear my dad's mouth about me being only sixteen. At seventeen, I was able to drive, and he'd better get used to be me being always gone and never home.

Boo was twenty years old and one of my father's workers. That man was fine as hell and had me turned on every time I saw him. My father didn't mix me with business, and that was a rule he never broke. However, at Paisley's baby shower, I ended up bumping into Boo. He had a wad of money in his hands to hand to Paisley for her baby. I was so in love when I laid eyes on this man, because he was all man. He was tall, slightly thick, and light skinned. He put me in the mind of Kevin Gates, and I'd let him eat the hell out my virgin booty. When he spoke, I got mesmerized by the gold grills in his mouth. Everything about Boo had me wanting to risk it all, but I couldn't come out and tell my father that I was dating one of his workers. He would kill me if he knew that I spent my weekends hanging with Boo.

Boo was willing to risk it all and tell my father, but I wasn't ready for him to be killed over me. My father wouldn't hesitate to kill Boo and make me watch so I would learn my lessons not to mess around with his workers. By day, I went to school and made sure my work was done, and by night, I hung out with Boo or was on the phone with him. I heard the door chime and took the phone off speakerphone.

"Girl, I'll talk to you later... my daddy just came through the door." I laughed when my father came into view.

"I'm sick of doing this shit with you, Paris."

"Girl, you kill me. I'll talk to you later." I hurried up and ended the call and placed my phone face down on the coffee table. "Hey, Daddy."

My father plopped down on the couch beside me and reached to pull me close so he could kiss me on the forehead. "Hey, baby girl. What you in here doing?"

"Homework and watching the news. They found some man stuffed in a mattress in front of some real estate office."

"Word? Nigga probably fucked with the wrong people." He shrugged like it was nothing. "How was your day?"

"It was good. I got some acceptance letters." I pulled them out of my Gucci messenger bag. "Look." I handed it to him.

He opened the Spellman packet and read a little before a huge smile appeared on his face. "My girl got into Spellman... You gonna make me get a Spellman sticker on my Benz?" He smirked and pulled me over to him with his free hand.

"Now read the other one."

He read it over and his smile got even bigger. "Columbia? Nah, you going here, Paris. I was sold on Atlanta but being that you got into a good school here, stay home."

"Daddyyyyyy!" I squealed in laughter. "I haven't decided what I'm doing yet. I'm still thinking about what school I want to go to."

"Paris, I'm proud as fuck of you. I know shit been crazy these past few months with the family and then me and Remi, but you held it down. I don't ever have to worry about you because you make sure your work is done and shit is on point. If I haven't told you before, I'm proud of you, baby girl."

"Awe, thanks, Daddy. I know you have a lot on your plate, so I try not to add more onto your plate. How do you feel about the new baby?"

"Excited as fuck. I can't wait to be a father again. I'm just wishing I get my baby boy."

"Awe, a little brother would be so cute. Me and Remi are going out shopping and lunch this weekend to catch up."

"Y'all always on the damn phone. What the hell you need to catch up with her about?"

"Girly stuff."

"Yeah, ight."

"The real tea is that you need to bring Remi home. I miss her being here, Dad." I missed Remi being home, but I knew that she needed to get her mind right. The fights had got so bad that they were doing it in front of me. A few times I saw her crying in the closet when she thought I wasn't near. The older I got, the more I realized that being grown wasn't the answer to everything. Once you were grown, you had a whole other host of problems that needed to be solved.

"Baby girl, trust, I'm working on that shit." He laughed.

"You're the king of Harlem... you can make anything happen."

"Baby, you're the princess of Harlem; you'll see that the people that mean the most aren't that easy to obtain with a snap of the finger.

"I love you, Daddy." I hugged him and then gathered all my books and cell phone. I stared at my phone and there was a text message from Boo. A smirk spread across my face. You'll just have to find out what happens in *A Rose In Harlem: Harlem King's Princess.*

EPILOGUE

MANIC

A Few Months Later....

"Yo, Doc, you sure she gonna snap back, because the way my daughter came out that shit... I'm not sure."

"Even though she pushed an eight-pound baby through her vaginal canal, everything will go back to normal. She must heal first," the doc informed as I held my daughter in my hand.

"Mitchell, can you stop with the questions," Paisley begged. "And give me my baby," she demanded.

We were at the baby's first doctor appointment, and Paisley was all swollen and shit. I couldn't complain; she pushed my baby girl out like a champ. Ight, she cried and shit, but she was a champ in my eyes. While we were expecting our baby to be born premature, my girl was overdue, and she was eight pounds and six ounces. Aubree Sundae was here, and she looked like her damn mother. Each little expression she made, she looked exactly like her mother. I was so hype to have my second daughter here and healthy. We worried her entire pregnancy, and God swooped in and showed us that he had the both of us and our baby girl covered. Man, being a parent felt like everything to me. Having small eyes looking up at me like I was their hero was the best thing in the world. I didn't give a fuck about anyone's opinion except my fucking kids.

Nisha had my daughter, Autumn Jade, and she was my little chunky pie. Shit, when you became a parent, you started making up dumb ass nicknames and didn't know where the fuck you pulled them from. Nisha was still on that bullshit, so we were going to court. She still couldn't get over that me and Paisley had got engaged at her baby shower. I told her that she wasn't about to have my baby out here looking stupid, and now her ass was the one looking like a fucking fool. She played games with me seeing my daughter, and Paisley had to stop me a few times from making sure she went missing. Now that I was a father, I didn't play about my kids, and you weren't about to use our personal issues to hold my child away from me. I think she was getting the hint, because when I climbed through her window at four in the morning, snatched my daughter, and told her ass if she called the cops I would kill her, she learned that I wasn't to be fucked with.

Courts couldn't stop me from seeing my kid, and I'd be damned if she thought she was going to the same. She was mad because I stopped bankrolling her life, and I was forcing her ass to get a job. Paisley didn't like that I was paying her so much money and since we were going to be married, she wanted to know where *our* money was going. When she took charge and called shit *ours,* a nigga felt all good and shit. I finally felt like I had a fucking family to love me. When she found out the full price of that baby shower and the twelve grand I was paying Nisha a month, she put a stop to it. Instead of twelve bands, I send her twenty-five hundred a month for my daughter. Along with the money, I make sure that all the newest clothes, bottles, pampers, and wipes were delivered like clockwork from me. Nisha felt like I was letting Paisley run my life, and we always fought about the shit. The moment she took me to court and wanted to get child support was the day that she fucked up with me. Even with all the other shit she had been pulling, she could still call me and tell me she needed me, and I would come running.

The moment she decided to step into court, the place I'd been my entire childhood , and try to get more money for my kid was the day she died to me. She couldn't ask me for shit, and if it didn't have shit to do with my child, she knew not to call me. I had one of the best family court lawyers, and he said I could get full custody of my child. I was with it and ready to go and get blood in court, but Paisley stopped me. She told me that despite the bullshit that Nisha was on, taking a child from their mother was wrong. If Nisha was neglecting my child, it would be one thing, but Nisha was a good ass mother. My daughter was always cleaned, dressed, and fed. Shit, she was too fed because she was like a damn butterball. She told me that we both needed to remove our personal feelings out and do that was right for our child. So I stopped trying to get full custody and did split custody.

Other than that shit, me and Paisley were good. Sayana was good too and loving being a big sister. The way she loved on Aubree, I knew they would be close once they both got older. Seeing Paisley be a mother to both those little girls warmed my heart. It was like she found her calling and knew what she was doing. Soon as Aubree came out, she took control, and her maternal instincts kicked in. We moved into our new place, and we loved that shit. What I loved the most was going upstairs and borrowing toilet tissue from Sundae and Grizz. They got so pissed when I came upstairs and took rolls of toilet tissue from them. Meanwhile, I had a bunch of rolls in my own closet. Fucking with them was the most funniest shit ever.

Sundae and Grizz were doing good. Even though they were back together, they were now doing couple's therapy together. Sundae had been trying to talk him into going to some Costa Rica couple's retreat, and he wasn't with it. Since she'd traveled, she got the bug, and now she wanted to go everywhere. Grizz was saying no now, but he wasn't about to let her out his sight ever again. Those three months they went without talking was the worst time in his life. So if she said they were going to the fucking moon, that nigga would be strapping up and going. As for puppy ashes, I mean Teyanna, she wasn't going to be a problem any longer. Even though it took Grizz years to do what should have been done, it was finally done.

Tweeti and Jah were still going strong. Dakota's body was found in Delaware under an under pass. Between Taz, the twins, and the new dog they'd just gotten, they were busy as hell. Jah was back doing physical therapy. Nothing could keep my nigga down, and he was about to be walking real soon. He was more determined now to get back up on his legs and walk like he was doing before. Evelyn had moved into her own apartment a few minutes from their house. She had a boyfriend she had met at her little meetings, and they had been going strong. She had just introduced him to Tweeti and Remi. Even with her moving out on her own, she still was there for Taz every morning. Tweeti and Jah were working on making a little girl that they wanted to name Yaz. It was short for Yazmin. I couldn't wait because if Tweeti came over to my house one more time to smell my damn baby, I was gonna have to get a restraining order on her.

Remi was still pregnant, and she and Uzi were expecting a baby boy. She was finally excited to be experiencing pregnancy. All she did was call everyone and tell us about the smallest shit that was happening with her body. I mean, we were all excited about her having a baby, but damn, I shouldn't hear about shit that only her nigga should be knowing. All she and Paisley did was sit on the phone and talk about the shit about pregnancy people didn't tell you. Like Paisley started losing some of her hair. She told Remi, and she started having a damn panic attack, and we had to drive to her crib to calm her down. Why the fuck was I driving to calm her down? Remi and Uzi were back together but not living together. They decided that they didn't want to move right in because Uzi was thinking about selling his brownstone. With Paris talking about getting her own place after graduation, he was considering getting a place out of Harlem for him, Remi, and the baby to move into.

I still couldn't believe that he was considering letting Paris get a place in the city. Shit, let Aubree or Autumn ask for a damn place at seventeen. Hell nah, I'm raising hell, and they getting beat with my belt. It was Uzi's daughter, and I didn't get involved because I would go the fuck off if somebody told me how to raise my child.

Emory and Shad were well... Emory and Shad. He had his little side chick, and she had her little boy toy. Shit worked for the both of them, and nobody tried to get to understand them. Tweeti and Emory still didn't get along but tolerated each other when the family got together. I didn't think that they would ever have a good relationship. Qua and Wynner were expecting another baby. Wynner and Paisley did playdates with the girls, but Paisley said she was sick of her trying to tell her how to be a parent, so their dates had slowed up some. Me and Wynner met a few times, but I didn't get involved with her ass. Qua was my nigga and I went to his shop to get my hair cut and chopped it up with him every week. Since the nigga left the game, he was boring as hell. He seemed unhappy if you asked me, but that wasn't my business.

Me and Paisley were planning our dream wedding. I couldn't wait to marry this woman. It was so much about her that I loved and made me excited to marry her. We were having issues with the planning because she wanted to control every damn thing. Shit, I wanted to fucking have some choice in the color and shit. Paisley's mother finally ended the relationship with her nigga. She thought her mother had finally found the light, but her mother went back to him a month later. She wasn't invited to the wedding, and she hadn't seen her granddaughter yet. I didn't push shit when it came to her with her mother. All in all, I was happy that I finally got the chick on Fulton Street that always ignored the shit out of me. It was crazy how life was, and my dream girl had my daughter and became my dream fiancée. Not to mention, she was *In Love With An East Coast Maniac.*

THE END
Make sure to join and follow me on all my social media to stay in loop of all things me!
Make sure you answer the questions asked!

www.facebook.com/JahquelJ
http://www.instagram.com/_Jahquel
http://www.twitter.com/Author_Jahquel
Be sure to join my reader's group on Facebook
www.facebook.com/ Jahquel's we reading or nah?

Make sure you join my newest group –
www.facebook.com/Babeswithbooks

COMING 10/17!

CPSIA information can be obtained
at www.ICGtesting.com
Printed in the USA
LVHW021732071218
599658LV00003B/334/P